# RAIDER

## WOLF CREEK
## FEUD

J.D. HARDIN

NOV -- 2013

BERKLEY BOOKS, NEW YORK

WOLF CREEK FEUD

A Berkley Book/published by arrangement with
the author

PRINTING HISTORY
Berkley edition/August 1988

ISBN: 0-425-10985-2

A BERKLEY BOOK ® TM 757,375
Berkley Books are published by the Berkley Publishing Group,
200 Madison Avenue, New York, NY 10016.
The name "BERKLEY" and the "B" logo
are trademarks belonging to the Berkley Publishing Corporation.

PRINTED IN THE UNITED STATES OF AMERICA

10  9  8  7  6  5  4  3  2  1

# CHAPTER ONE

Gavin Dowling and his two pards let their horses set their own pace through the wide green sea of prairie grass. It was early morning, and the sun was still low in the eastern sky, but they could feel its blazing heat already through their flannel shirts and denims. From time to time the men tilted their hats to keep the brim shading their eyes. They rode easy in the saddle—all three had spent far more of their lives sitting in a saddle than they ever had on a chair.

"Gonna be a bitch," Gavin commented, with a sideways nod toward the sun.

Neither of the other two argued with him on this. A stranger might have thought they hadn't heard him, since neither shifted his eyes or moved a muscle in his face. But they heard him all right. If they hadn't gone along with what he said, they'd have let him know then and there.

They rode north over the huge empty Kansas grasslands, keeping their eyes on the far horizon in front of them. All three were gaunt, unshaven, grim-faced. They had spent the past four nights sleeping under the stars, finding a waterhole, and shooting prairie chickens to eat. This riding and thirsting and starving had dried them out after their blast in Newton, which had lasted a week or maybe ten days. That cow town would remember them awhile.

But they had paid good money for their fun there, and left without owing anyone a cent. They had even paid to bury the man they killed—a nice pine coffin, a little picket fence around the grave, and an ornamental plank marker with angels and things scorched into it with hot metal, along with the man's name. No one knew who he was, but he had been kind of thin, and the barkeep recalled him saying something about Denver, so the marker read: Colorado Slim, Blessed with the Lord, Respected among Men.

It hadn't been out of the goodness of their hearts or from pangs of guilt that they had paid to bury the man. The marshal had insisted on it. Since he had let them win the argument about it being a fair shooting in self-defense, they had felt obligated to let him win the argument about who was going to pay for Boot Hill. All three being very drunk at the time, they had sent Colorado Slim off in better style than the bastard deserved, with a valid preacher saying words from the Good Book. It was on extravagances like this that they had blown their money.

"Easy come, easy go," Gavin Dowling liked to say.

The money had come easy enough—$1,200 in ten-dollar gold pieces, courtesy of the Kansas & Topeka Railroad. They had robbed the train at a coaling station, without bothering the passengers, taking only the sole strongbox in the freight cars, a mine payroll. They had ridden for three days with the money, then blown it in Newton. Now they were riding again.

Gavin called it discipline—riding for days with gold pieces in their saddlebags, ignoring temptation, until they were far enough from the robbery to deny they had anything to do with it. Most gunslicks and thieves headed for the nearest town to spend their loot. Anyone looking for them didn't have to search far. They had left Newton penniless. Now they were riding again. Gavin knew where they were going. He had been born north of the Kansas state line, in Nebraska. He knew where he was going.

"There they are," he called finally.

The other two men rode for twenty minutes more before they too could make out the line of telegraph poles stretching across the prairie in the distance. They couldn't see any rails, but Western Union strung its lines along railroad right-of-ways, and Gavin knew that trains ran here.

When they finally got to them, the tracks weren't much to look at—a single pair of rails laid on crosswise pine ties. No engineers had had to work on a roadbed with banking or inclines for these trains. The track layers had just dropped the timber ties on the grass, spiked the rails to them, and moved right along.

The three men rode beside the tracks for some miles until they came to a low swell in the ground. The water table was lower here, and the sun had killed the grass everywhere, leaving it standing yellow and brittle.

"Nice place," Gavin Dowling said admiringly.

It would suit their purpose fine. They could see

along the tracks for many miles each way, so they would have plenty of notice of a train coming. The men dismounted and stood in the shade of their horses. The sun beat down. Nothing moved. Not even flies came out at this time of day on the prairie.

As the train sped westward across northern Kansas, the cars gently rocked from side to side. The passengers were having a smooth ride over the gentle undulations of the prairie. One man lay stretched on a bench seat, softly snoring under the black hat tipped down over his face. He wore a black shirt, sunbleached denims, and battered calfskin riding boots. On the luggage rack above him were a pair of beatup saddlebags, a scuffed black leather jacket, and a carbine. While he slept, his right hand rested casually on the plain wood grips of the big Remington .44 six-gun in the holster on his right hip.

"You're seeing the real thing in this one, a real genuine gunfighter if I ever laid eyes on one," a short, stout, cheerful man said in an uncharacteristically low voice to a group of passengers. They were Easterners, west of the Mississippi for the first time, and the short, stout man had appointed himself their guide on all things western. "If any one of you don't believe me, just try walking over and touching him. Before your fingers make contact, he'll have whipped out that gun of his and drilled a hole in you—even before he wakes up. By the time that hat falls off his face, you'll be standing before the Judgment Seat of your Maker."

"That's certainly something I want to postpone as long as possible," a prosperous-looking banker type said.

The others laughed, but not loud enough to chance waking up the sleeping desperado. They had been taking furtive looks at him since he had boarded the train back in Independence, Missouri. He had ignored them, politely declining conversation. He stared out the windows for long periods of time, slept, or paced up and down the car like a caged lion. He was not someone to whom they would wish to serve tea in their parlors, but he had an undeniable aura of swift violent action about him. They could easily imagine him taking part in some horrible event, one of those lurid happenings in the wilderness about which eastern newspapers loved to give detailed gory accounts. It was almost as if, just by being near him, they themselves were partaking in some of the danger—at a safe distance, of course. But how safe? An unpredictable brute like this might kill them all in their sleep for the small change they possessed. The ladies shivered deliciously at this prospect, because it was undeniable that this gunfighter was very handsome, with jet black eyes, a tanned face, and long black mustaches.

After a while, the sleeping man stirred, yawned, stretched, and climbed to his feet. When the banker type suggested that the gunman join him for a coffee, the latter said no thanks and reached up to the saddlebags on the luggage rack. He pulled out a full bottle of whiskey and then took down the carbine. One woman became faint, having decided that this was the point where he would murder them all. Instead the big gunfighter—he was six-two in his boots—put his hat on his head and walked to the end of the car, bottle in left hand and carbine in right.

Between the cars, he climbed the brakeman's ladder to the car roof. A young brakeman was reading a newspaper in the cool breeze, his legs dangling over the rear edge of the roof.

"You can't come up here," he said.

"Who says?"

"Railroad regulations."

"Regulations ain't nothing without someone to enforce them," the gunman climbing the ladder informed him.

"I'm a brakeman. I ain't the guard."

"Then shut your mouth," the gunman advised.

He climbed up on the roof and sat on its side. His heels suddenly appearing at the top of a window surprised some passengers beneath. He pulled the cork from the whiskey bottle, took a deep draft, and held out the bottle to the brakeman.

"No, thank you kindly, sir. I take my responsibilities seriously."

The gunman nodded approvingly.

The train sped on over the rolling prairie. The two men sat in silence, the brakeman reading and the gunslinger staring out over the flatlands, occasionally slugging whiskey, easy and contented up here in a way it was impossible for him to be in the confines of the railroad car's interior.

The young brakeman looked up quickly when he heard the metallic scrape of a shell being levered into the carbine's chamber.

"Grass fire up ahead," the gunman said.

The brakeman stuffed the newspaper in his back pocket and moved to the brake wheel. A big plume of white smoke rose against the blue sky, with an orange patch of blazing grass at its base, some miles ahead along the line. Being the mid-train brakeman, he signaled with arm waves to the brakeman at the front cars and the one at the back. The front brakeman tried to catch the engineer's or fireman's attention in the locomotive. At their lower level, they wouldn't have seen the fire yet.

The fireman was shoveling coal into the locomotive's boiler, and the engineer could not hear the brakeman's shouts. It was some minutes before the engineer turned around and caught sight of him. He then peered out the side of his cab before deciding to lower the locomotive's head of steam. The three brakemen twisted the brake wheels, and the train gradually slowed.

By now the locomotive was near the grass fire. A carpet of orange flames danced fifteen feet high, maybe a mile long and a quarter wide.

"We can't run this one," the mid-train brakeman said in alarm. "The heat maybe's twisted the rails— we'll jump the tracks and be roasted slowly alive."

The engineer reached the same conclusion at about the same time. He signaled to the front brakeman, who signaled to the other two. All three twisted down hard on the brake wheels. The steel car wheels locked and screeched as they were dragged on the steel rails. The train came to a full stop about a quarter mile from the grass fire.

Three horsemen appeared from behind the cover of the smoke and began eating up the distance between them and the train.

The engineer frantically signaled to the brakemen to release the brakes. As the brake wheels were spun, he threw the locomotive in reverse and shunted backward. But the locomotive had lost its head of steam, and its progress was slow. The three horsemen were gaining on it. They would catch up with it before the train could work up enough speed to outrun the horses.

The gunman on the car roof tipped back his black hat from his face, lay belly down, and squinted along the sights of his carbine. He centered the bead of the front sight snugly in the notch of the rear sight, then followed the blue shirt of the lead rider with the bead and squeezed home the trigger. The shot lifted the dude out of the saddle and dumped him on his head in the grass.

The hooves of the second horse pummeled the fallen man like a rag doll, finishing off whatever work the bullet had left undone.

The two remaining riders sent a fusillade of shots in the direction of the man on the car roof. The brakeman ducked down on his ladder between the cars as bullets whined through the air. The big man with the carbine showed his indifference to their marksmanship by standing up and taking a toke on his whiskey bottle.

When he raised the carbine to his shoulder, the two horsemen broke away and rode like hell for the horizon. The train began to slow in its backward motion. As it came to a stop, the big man ran back along the car roofs, leaping from one to another, until he came to a freight car. Once the train halted, he clambered down a ladder and joined the train guard in unlatching and lowering the door of the freight car, which served as a ramp for a saddled horse to step down. By prearrangement, the guard had saddled the horse once trouble started. The big man leaped on the horse's back, spurred the animal, and took off over the grassland after the two robbers.

As he rode after the two men, Raider was exultant. He had recognized one rider as one of the Dowling brothers, all three of whom were train raiders in Kansas and Missouri. He wasn't sure which Dowling this one was, but Raider was willing to settle for any of the three. He had been riding trains for three weeks now, hoping to get a crack at them. The railroads had banded together in hiring a group of Pinkerton operatives to fight the robbers. Raider was part of this group, but unlike the others, he worked alone. Allan Pinkerton, founder and head of the Pinkerton National Detective Agency, tolerated the vagaries of his star operative. He knew that he had to, because Raider did what he goddamn pleased, no matter what anyone said or did.

The big Pinkerton cursed at his lazy horse and urged it on in pursuit of the two riders. He was gaining on them, because his horse was fresh and well rested. Although they had been given a start on him, they hadn't used it to full advantage, not expecting to be pursued by a horseman from the train. Even now, they were none too worried—it was still two against one, in their favor.

As Raider neared them, the two horsemen turned in their saddles and fired back with their revolvers. They had little hope of hitting him, but he and his horse together made a big target. Any bullet that found its mark anywhere on this target would stop him. The robbers reloaded as they rode, then turned in the saddle again to loose off their guns' six chambers. A couple of the bullets came close enough this time to make Raider decide he wasn't going to give them any more chances. He stood in the stirrups to steady himself against his galloping horse, raising the carbine to his right shoulder, and sighted along its barrel at the back of the nearest rider.

Raider didn't feel a thing. He just grew aware he was sliding sideways off his horse. Figuring he was hit, he disregarded everything except concentrating on one last shot. He aimed the carbine at the rider's back, squeezed the trigger, and slumped down to bite the dust.

The sunbaked ground beneath the grass was hard as rock. When Raider hit it—he was a big man, and he hit it hard—it jarred every bone in his body. He took the fall squarely on his back and lay where he fell, winded and slightly stunned. He waited for the pain of the gunshot to begin, still not knowing in what part of his body he had been hit. The shock from the bullet's impact sometimes delayed the pain like this. He twitched himself, expecting at any moment to experience the searing agony that he was all too familiar with. But nothing happened. His bones ached from the fall—another sensation he was familiar with. That was all.

Then he saw the saddle on the grass near him. The brass buckle of the saddle's belly band was disconnected. He had fallen from his horse not because he had been shot but because he had slid off along with the saddle.

Raider jumped to his feet, cursing the railroad guard, who had saddled the horse for him. The man might have been in league with the train robbers and

have done it deliberately. More likely, he was a tow-
nee scared of being kicked by the horse or crushed by
it against the car wall as he cinched the saddle girth
under its belly.

The Pinkerton saw the remaining robber on horseback growing smaller on the horizon. Two miles or
so behind him, the train had begun to move forward
again. His horse and those of the two downed bandits
were running together, stopping to graze a moment,
then running again, celebrating their newfound free-
dom.

Picking up his carbine, he walked a couple of
hundred yards to the bandit he had shot while sliding
off his horse. He had shattered the man's spinal cord
just below the base of the neck. Raider looked at the
dead man's face. This was not one of the Dowling
brothers. Too bad.

Moving slowly toward them, he tried to approach
the horses. They let him get within twenty yards of
them before running. They stopped again a few
hundred yards off, began grazing, and appeared not
to notice his approach—until he was within twenty
yards of them, when they would run again, stop
again, and let him approach again. Raider tired of the
game before the horses did.

He looked around him. The single horseman had
disappeared to the north, the train to the west, the
grass fire having burned low enough for it to pass.
He started hollering cusses as loud as his voice
would carry.

Raider had no water and no food, but this was not
what he was cussing about. He had left a two-thirds-
full whiskey bottle on that goddamn train car roof.

# CHAPTER TWO

The first thing Simon Carter and his two nephews noticed when they rode into Bladen was a bunch of Dowlings standing on Main Street. The three Carter men didn't want trouble, but they weren't going to be scared off, either. They had as much right to be in the town of Bladen as the Dowlings. They rode along, without a word to one another, just like there was nothing to worry about and none of those Dowlings were there.

The Carters and Dowlings were blood enemies. The two warring clans operated cattle ranches out by Wolf Creek, a three-hour ride from Bladen, which was in Webster County, southern Nebraska, between the Platte and Republican rivers. The Dowlings hailed from New York State and were proud Yankees. The Carters came from South Carolina's Low Country, and they taught their sons never to forget the Confederacy's ruin.

Simon Carter missed the fistfight that had just taken place. He and his two nephews had not seen

Abner Dowling square off with Elijah Carter, as the other Dowlings stood and watched, knowing they had no need to help out Abner in this match. They had not seen hammer-fisted Abner Dowling beat their cousin Elijah Carter senseless and then steal his six-gun from its holster as he lay on the ground. All they saw was Abner Dowling with the six-gun in his hand, standing along with a bunch of his clan over the prone figure of their cousin. Naturally they figured there had been gunplay and the Dowlings had shot Elijah Carter dead.

Now, Simon Carter and his two nephews didn't want no trouble with Dowlings while they were in the town of Bladen, but that didn't include standing idly by and seeing their own kith and kin murdered before their eyes. Simon didn't have to say a word to his two nephews. Right about the same time, all three men, still on horseback, dove for their guns.

Simon Carter fired at Abner Dowling, missed him, and brought down another Dowling standing behind him. Abner used the gun in his hand to blow one of the Carter nephews out of the saddle before being struck in the gut himself by Simon Carter's second bullet. Simon and his surviving nephew plugged two more Dowlings, while three more hightailed it through the batwing doors of the nearest saloon. They were not cowards. They were unarmed and wanted to survive so they could fight on another day.

When the gunsmoke cleared, six men lay on Bladen's dusty Main Street—two Carters and four Dowlings.

"Two of them for every one of us," Simon Carter

said to his nephew, stuffing fresh cartridges into his smoking revolver.

Simon was a mite surprised to see his cousin Elijah stand up and shake his head to clear it. "Where am I? Yeah, I remember. That son of a bitch Abner Dowling whupped me because I laughed at his glass eye."

"Ain't Abner who has the glass eye," the nephew corrected him. "That's Abner's brother."

"Well, sure made Abner mad anyhow," Elijah said.

"You're a damn fool, boy," Simon told him sternly. "You just brought on a new wave of trouble. You help your cousin tie my nephew's body on his horse, mount up behind him, and be leaving town along with us. You here alone?"

"Yes, sir." Elijah picked up his six-gun from where it lay next to Abner's body. Abner was still breathing and moaning and threshing about. "You want me to finish off the coyote?" Elijah asked.

"You done enough for one day," Simon snapped. "Now do what I told you. Way I see it, Abner don't have too much time left to him in Nebraska anyhow, bleeding from the gut the way he is."

No one tried to stop the Carters from leaving town. So long as you weren't a Dowling or a Carter or married to one of their girls, their affairs were something you kept your nose out of. So far as the marshal and sheriff were concerned, the more Dowlings and Carters killed by one another in their blood feud, the fewer would be left in Webster County. The townspeople let them ride out in silence toward Wolf Creek.

• • •

"What are we going to do now?" Emma Carter asked Everett Dowling.

"Run."

"I can't, Ev. I got to look out for my Aunt Janie."

"Let some of the others care for her. There's plenty of them."

"I promised," she said in that voice which he knew already meant it was final.

Everett Dowling loved this Carter girl, even though he could plainly see she too had that hard, wild streak most of the Carters had. It wasn't difficult to guess why he had taken a fancy to her, in spite of her being a Carter—she was the prettiest girl in the whole of Webster County, and maybe in all Nebraska, too. Leastways that was Everett's opinion.

"That old aunt of yours could live another twenty years," he complained, "and our two families ain't going to soften none in all that time. Either side would prefer to see us dead rather than married. We're going to be old people ourselves by the time we live together."

"You said these ranches ain't going to last but a few years more, Ev, with all them settlers stringing wire across the rangelands."

His attention was immediately diverted. "You know what I seen yesterday, just ten miles east of here? Corn! Some Dutchman had plowed up the grass, strung wire all around, and was growing this stuff on the rangeland. If us and you Carters had any sense, we'd be burning his house and trampling his corn instead of fighting one another. It don't make no sense for us remaining ranchers to be killing each other while those settlers are sweeping west like a swarm of locusts, fencing off the public rangelands to grow their crops. We only got a few years left before they swarm over us at Wolf Creek."

"Maybe we can get married then," Emma said hopefully.

"I can't wait that long," Everett said tensely.

"Why not?" Emma batted her eyes at him. "Ain't I giving you all the benefits a married man is entitled to?"

Everett smiled and reached out a hand to touch her breast.

"Don't. People will see."

He laughed. "If anyone was to see us now, they'd be more struck by me and you being a Dowling and a Carter than by anything we were doing with each other. Anyway, no one's going to find us here in the long grass of this hollow."

She let herself be calmed and caressed by him. Then she got hot and pushed him on his back in the grass. She unbuckled his belt, unbuttoned his fly, and pulled his pants down over his hips. She used her fingers and lips to arouse his cock.

She licked his belly button, kissed his belly, stroked her face and neck with his cock. He felt his balls being cradled in the palm of her hand as she tongued the length of his stiff shaft.

He felt her forefinger and thumb circle his cock and move up and down it in time to her lips sucking its head. He drove his dick deep into her throat and heard her gasp for breath between his thrusts.

When she could take no more, she rolled away from him, hitched up her dress and petticoats, moaning unintelligibly to him.

He pulled his pants clear of his ankles and lay on top of her, between her legs. He guided his straining

cock into the soft slit of her sex, then heaved forward
with the full force of his manhood into her trembling
warmth.

Folk out on Wolf Creek buried their dead in Bladen's
cemetery, went to Bladen's church, and sent their
children to school there. These were some of the reasons why the town was neutral territory for the two
clans. But it had always been an uneasy truce. No
one knew what to expect now. It was up to the
Dowlings, the Carters said, because they had lost
only one man and the Dowlings had lost four. If anyone was going to be looking for vengeance, it would
be the Dowlings.

The day of the burials, the marshal ordered the
saloons closed all morning and afternoon. He "kindly
requested" both clans to stay out of town after the
funerals, and deputized two dozen assistant marshals
to show he meant what he said.

No one knew what might happen if the two clans
met at the cemetery. Neither family held with the
preachings of the town's clergyman, so he would not
be there to quiet things down. The marshal said he
hoped they'd all finally finish each other off where it
would be quick and simple to bury them where they
fell. He said he wasn't going to be there either, add-
ing that the residents of the town were more in need
of protection than the residents of Boot Hill.

The Dowlings got there early, having four separate funeral ceremonies to attend. The Carters came
late, figuring the Dowlings would be long finished
by then. But the Dowlings took their lamentations
seriously, and by the third funeral, things had slowed
to nearly a stop. They were still burying the fourth

man when the Carter wagon bearing the coffin came along the trail, followed by family members. The Carters had no wish to interrupt, but now that they were here, they were not willing to stand still or turn back. They went over to their side of the cemetery, carefully avoiding to stare at their enemies on the other side.

Family members read prayers over the open grave. Some of the Carter men, feeling that they were being drowned out by the Dowling prayers, raised their voices to a good high volume. One Carter man mentioned "cold-blooded assassins," and another "Godless barbarians." The Dowlings yelled "Southern trash" and "murdering horse thieves." The men would have opened fire on each other there and then had it not been for the women and children mixed up among them. They went back to the task of burying their dead more quietly but not more peacefully, for it was a tense sort of quietness that everyone knew would end in an outburst.

The Dowlings left the cemetery first. Some were still gathered a short distance from the gate when the Carters began to stream out. Nothing might have happened if Simon Carter hadn't made a point of advancing some steps alone toward the Dowling group, with a contemptuous look on his face, as if he dared any of them to step forward and meet him.

His challenge, if it was one, did not go unmet. A youth of no more than sixteen broke away from the Dowling group. He had tousled hair and wore a long, tattered coat that flapped around his legs.

Simon stood and watched him come, hoping maybe to back out with a few words peacefully from what he had started. The youth pulled a sawed-off double-barrel shotgun from under his coat, snapped back the hammers, and, firing from his hip, gave Simon Carter both barrels. The left and right loads of buckshot gouged craters out of each side of Simon's chest.

When his cousin Elijah saw him fall a victim of this sneak attack, he hauled his Peacemaker from its holster and blasted two shots into the youth before he could either reload or run back to join his family.

Elijah Carter had been ashamed of his role the previous day. Now he stood tall with a smoking gun and a dead Dowling in front of him. He walked a few paces forward to give the Dowlings a good look at him.

Two women pulled him back into the family group. As in the graveyard, it was only their presence among them, along with that of the children, that prevented a full-scale shoot-out.

The Dowlings held back several of their men from challenging Elijah.

"Easy there, lads," old Thady Dowling said. "We'll need you to look after things till Gavin gets home, or either of his brothers, Arthur or Martin. One or more of them is bound to show real soon. Them are the men to gut those Carter bastards alive. There'll be skin and hair flying when them boys come home."

# CHAPTER THREE

"Ain't no liquor in this town, mister," the man told Raider outside the feed store.

"I guess I'm still in Kansas, then."

"You sure are. State line is a couple of hours to the north of here."

Kansas was by law a dry state, though it would have been hard to guess this in any of the cow towns, where the saloons, gaming halls, and brothels were open twenty-four hours a day. But this place was north and east of the big cattle drives and was dry as a bone.

Handing the man three wanted sheets with a drawing of a Dowling brother's face on each, Raider asked, "Any of these men pass through here in the last day or so?"

The man unhesitatingly picked the one showing Gavin Dowling. "Five thousand dollars reward, dead or alive . . . Not bad. Not bad. I could have snuck up behind him and shot him dead. Hell, no. I'd have chickened out. He looked too mean and jumpy and fast, know what I'm saying? He spent the night down at the rooming house, left without paying first thing this morning, saying he'd be back. He ain't coming back here. Rode north out of town. You a lawman? You don't look like no lawman to me. A bounty hunter is my guess. I don't mind telling you, fella, you're gonna have to earn your reward when you catch up with this one. He's a real rattlesnake."

"'Preciate your information. Know where I can get a meal?"

"You aiming to pay for it?"

"In gold, if I have to."

"One silver dollar will buy you all you can eat and a pot of fine coffee, too. You go over to that house painted yaller there and say I sent you."

"Much obliged."

At the eating house, it wasn't hard to bring the subject of conversation around to the stranger who had left town without paying for his night's stay. It came as no surprise to them to see his face on a wanted sheet. They more or less repeated what the man on the street had said. Having watered and fed his three horses some oats, Raider was ready to hit the saddle again when he was approached by a young man with fair hair and mustaches.

He said to Raider, "I'm told you're hunting down Gavin Dowling. He rob a train or steal horses or just kill somebody?"

"Maybe one or the other or all three."

"It figures," the young man said. "I know where he's headed. Latrobe. It's a town north of here, over the state line in Nebraska, about four hours' ride."

"What's he doing there?"

"The Dowlings like that town. He's got family there."

"I thought he hailed from Webster County," Raider said. "I reckoned he might be heading there."

"Not if he thinks he has someone on his trail. He'll stop in Latrobe and rid himself of you."

"How come you know so much about him?" Raider asked.

"I come from Wolf Creek, not far from where he does."

"Did Gavin see you while he was in town?"

The fair-haired young man smiled. "I wouldn't be standing talking with you if he had."

"What's he got against you?"

"I'm a Carter."

Raider figured he was maybe six hours behind Gavin Dowling. This was good, considering how he had started out. Having been left alone on the prairie with a dead man and three loose horses, Raider had tried to catch the horses in darkness. Their sense of smell and skittishness proved too much for him. Next morning, after a few hours of sleep on the grass, he was thinking of trekking back to the railroad line to catch a ride on the next train when his horse led the two others to him. The sun was up, they were thirsty, and could find no water. Within minutes they were nuzzling him, wanting to be friends. Raider told them they were no-good sons of bitches who deserved to die. His horse stood meekly while Raider saddled him. He hitched the other two behind him and rode three hours before finding a waterhole. By then, he just stuck his head into the water along with theirs.

Riding north all that day, he changed mounts frequently. He shot a prairie chicken and slept the night at a waterhole. He hit the dry town on his second day of pursuit, and he kept switching between the three horses. He hoped to make Latrobe by sundown, have two meals in one day, a few drinks, and maybe even sleep in a bed.

On the previous day, he had seen occasional bunches of cattle but no cowhands, and he hadn't happened across a ranch house. This day he was luckier—or the land was more thickly settled. Occasional riders steered him on his way, and he stopped by two ranch houses to water his horses. At one place, the foreman was talkative and offered him coffee.

"Been a few years since I rode up this way from Kansas," Raider told him. "I don't rightly recall when exactly it was, but it wasn't all that long ago. But I see big changes. You'd still come across Pawnee hunting parties back then, and there was buffalo everywhere. I ain't seen a single one or the other in the last two days."

The foreman nodded gravely. "This rangeland ain't what it used to be. Things are getting worse by the day. You come back here in another five years and you won't recognize the place. Them damn farmers will have the whole place ripped up. You were talking about Indians a moment ago. They say it's wrong to dig up the earth. Damn, I hate to have to agree with them on anything, but I'll go right along with them on that."

The ranch foreman scowled, and that was the end of hospitality there.

Raider pushed on and reached Latrobe well before

sundown. He stabled the three horses, found himself a hotel room, visited a barber for a shave, and walked across the street to a big saloon called Sam's Frontier. The place was nearly empty—Raider guessed it filled up with cowhands only on weekends. The few drinkers at the long bar decided him to give up his law-enforcement approach. None of these men looked like they might be keen to see law and order in Latrobe. Raider's big advantage was that he didn't look too law-abiding either.

He stood awhile with his whiskey bottle at the bar before curiosity caused one of the other drinkers to sidle up to him and put a few questions. The Pinkerton knew everyone in the almost silent saloon would be listening to his answers.

"You looking to buy a herd of beeves in these parts, mister? I know some fine buys if you are."

Raider smiled. He knew that the last thing he looked like was a prosperous cattleman wishing to make a purchase. "Naw, I ain't here for cows."

They digested that information in silence for a minute or so before the next question. "Ain't nothing much here 'cept cows. You ain't a farmer, are you?"

"No, I ain't a farmer."

"I'm mighty pleased to hear that," the man said. "Worse than varmints, them farmers. They ain't welcome here. Now, you may not know it by looking at me, but I'm a shrewd judge of a man. I could tell you things about a stranger just by looking at him. Would you believe that? No? Well, me and my pard down the bar had a dollar bet on you. I said you was here to stay because you had some purpose in mind in coming to Latrobe. He said you were just passing through and would go in the morning. Who won the bet?"

"You did," Raider said in a friendly way. "I came to meet someone here."

There was a definite stir of interest now.

"Maybe I know him," the man said, prompting him.

"Maybe you do. Gavin Dowling is his name."

There was a pause. "You a friend of his?"

"An old pard," Raider said with an easy smile.

They believed him, Raider could see that. He looked rough and tough enough to be a sidekick of Dowling's. The townsman laid off his questioning in a hurry, and grew vague real fast when Raider put questions to him. All the same, he indirectly answered the Pinkerton's inquiries through his reactions. There was no doubt in Raider's mind that this man had seen Gavin Dowling within a matter of hours and that he was scared to death of him. This fear extended now to Raider—all the man's barroom aggressiveness went up in smoke. He suddenly looked relieved when a heavyset young man with a broad scar on his right cheek walked in and bellied up to the bar.

"Stranger here's been asking for your cousin Gavin," the townsman told the heavyset young man, who gave Raider a suspicious look.

"You can tell the stranger he left town in a hurry on some important business."

The townsman said nothing. His work was done, and he could now sit back and enjoy himself while the stranger and the member of the Dowling clan sorted things out between them. Saloon fights were

the chief form of entertainment in the town of Latrobe.

Raider responded nice and easy. "I can't think of
nothing important round here for Gavin, unless he's
gone home to take care of those troublemakers who
bother you people. What do you call them? Carters?"

"My name is Brad Dowling. Who told you about
them?"

"They call me Raider. Gavin told me about
them."

"Hell, he never mentions their name," Brad spat
at him. "I'll tell you how you know. The country
south of here is crawling with renegade Carters. One
of them told you. But you're right, that's where my
cousin is gone. Our family needs his help bad."

"How come you ain't there to help too?" Raider
asked.

"I've had a little trouble in Webster County and I
can't go back for a spell. I don't mind telling you all
this, stranger, because you ain't going to be able to
put it to any use." He turned to the other men in the
saloon. "You know who this fella called Raider is? A
railroad detective. My cousin told me about him.
Gavin tried to rob a train, and this dude came out of
a freight car already mounted on a horse. He took my
cousin by surprise, but next thing his saddle slipped
off his horse—and him along with it!"

The men hooted at this. Not too many things were
held sacred in these parts, but horsemanship was one
of them. For a man to make a fool of himself in a bar
or in bed was easily forgiven, but not in a saddle.
There was only one way for Raider to settle this
deadly insult and that was in blood.

Instead, the Pinkerton smiled tolerantly, not bothering to deny anything. "Did your cousin mention what happened to the two men who rode along with him to rob that train?"

"No," Brad Dowling said, surprised. "I thought he was there alone."

Raider shood his head. "He left alone."

"Anyway it don't matter. Like I said, you ain't putting this information to any use. Gavin told me to watch out for you—just in case you ever managed to tie that saddle back on."

More hoots and hollers along the bar plus a round of drinks on Brad Dowling for everyone except Raider.

"I didn't buy you a drink on purpose, Raider, because I want you to have a clear head. I'm thinking you're going to need it in the next minute or so."

Raider answered in a low, calm voice. "I'm thinking you're a country boy who's in way over his head and don't even know it."

Raider was mistaken in believing that this might make Brad Dowling think twice about starting trouble. Instead, Raider's words only provoked him into showing what a fast gun he thought himself to be. He stalked along the bar, closing the short distance between him and Raider in a gunfighter's crouch.

Raider freed his hands, but otherwise he hardly responded in any way to the other man's threatening stance.

Brad stopped just short of Raider's arm reach, so he could not be hit by a fist. He told Raider to go for his gun. At this distance, it would be impossible to miss.

While Brad was still saying the words, Raider's

right hand streaked to the handle of his heavy, long-barrel .44 revolver.

The gun swung up from his holster in a blurred half arc. Only this time Raider did something different—he didn't thumb back the hammer as the barrel rose. Uncocked, the double-action Remington would not fire.

As the muzzle came level with Brad Dowling's face, Raider saw the frightened look dawn in his eyes—the look of a man who knows he has lost and must now pay the consequences. Brad's gun was clear of its leather, but the barrel was not raised and the hammer was not cocked. He now saw what Raider meant by a country boy in deeper than he understood—if he had chosen to do so, the Pinkerton could have blasted him before he managed to even point his six-gun.

With the muzzle of his gun almost touching Brad's nose, Raider flicked his wrist and brought the gun barrel smartly against Dowling's left temple. He went out like a light and slumped on the floor at Raider's feet.

"No point in killing a child," Raider said to the barkeep. Pointing to his whiskey bottle, he asked, "How much do I owe you for what I've drunk?"

Intending to get an early start for Webster County the next day, and likewise intending to avoid taking on a skinful of liquor and maybe some more hassles with members of the Dowling clan, Raider headed for his hotel. Thinking maybe he'd sleep better after a little loving, he stopped off on the way at another saloon. This place was lit with polished brass oil lamps, paintings of nudes hung on the walls, the tabletops were marble, and signs said that spitting was not allowed. It was the kind of fancy place that Raider normally avoided, except when he was in search of a woman. For some reason inexplicable to him, women liked this kind of place more than a simple, straightforward saloon where a drinker didn't have to worry about breaking the furniture or heaving a bottle at a mirror.

Kristin was a big-boned Swedish blonde, born in Minnesota, who had gone with her family as a child on the Oregon Trail and got stranded when every one of them but her died of cholera. Over the years, sort of homing eastward toward Minnesota, she found herself in Nebraska. It wasn't exactly on her way, but she was in no hurry and hadn't any fixed destination anyhow, since she couldn't recall the name of the Minnesota town she had left as a child. Raider wasn't much of a talker himself, but he made a good listener when someone had something to say. Kristin could see that he was interested in her as a real person, and it had been a while since she had met a man like that.

"I guess you're leaving tomorrow," she said.

"At first light," he confirmed.

"Then we don't have time to waste."

Together they headed toward the hotel. In his room, Raider unbuttoned her bodice and reached beneath her lace underthings to fondle her breasts. He played with her nipples and ran his fingertips over her smooth skin.

She sat on the edge of the big four-poster bed, slowly disrobing, while he sat beside her and softly stroked each new part of her body that she exposed to him. When she was naked, she pulled him toward her and helped him pull off his clothes. After his shirt, she undid the buckle of his belt, and his holstered gun fell to the floor. He kicked off his boots, removed his pants, and lay next to her on the bed, his body touching hers. He took deep pleasure in the warm silky feel of her body next to his. He fondled and stroked her until she grew passionate and begged him to enter her.

He thrust his great knob into her throbbing warmth and drove deep inside her. Her pelvis thrust against him, and she responded to the full force of his passion with her powerful hips. The four-poster creaked and shook under the ferocity of their efforts.

In spite of his vigorous rutting, Raider heard the shot from the room beneath. At the sound of a second gunshot, some plaster from the ceiling fell. It wasn't until the third shot that the Pinkerton realized that the bullets were ripping up through the floorboards of his room and embedding themselves in his ceiling.

Without withdrawing from Kristin, Raider reached down beside the bed for his gun and fired two shots down through the floorboards. He let his gun fall out of his hand and resumed pistoning into her.

Kristin was not so enthusiastic. "It's all right for you," she said. "I'm beneath and you're on top. I'm the one who'll get shot in the backside."

"Don't worry," Raider answered her, not missing a stroke, "the mattress is too thick."

"Aren't you going to find out who it is."

"Later," Raider grunted. "Right now I'm busy."

# CHAPTER FOUR

Gavin Dowling kept to some low hills to avoid the town of Bladen, hoping to arrive at Wolf Creek without being seen by any Carters or someone who might tell them he was here. He began to see familiar brands on the cattle and to recognize draws he had known since he was a boy. For some years now he had behaved himself in Webster County, being more interested in bigger scores elsewhere and wanting to keep his home turf as a haven from the law.

He figured that the railroad detective who had surprised him at the train robbery and killed his two pards might have recognized him. Railroad detectives were experts at that. If the man had put a name to him, he might guess he had come to Wolf Creek, where he was born. In all probability, he would not —railroad detectives were paid to guard trains, and they rarely wandered far from the line they were being paid to guard. However, just in case the detective had come after him, he had tipped off his cousin Brad in Latrobe. He hardly knew the kid, except to hear he was in some kind of trouble and had to cross the state line. Brad had been more than willing to show his big bad cousin that he now was a man too. Maybe the kid would come in useful. Maybe he'd get himself killed. Gavin didn't much care.

It was not love of his family that brought Gavin Dowling to Wolf Creek to face the Carters. He was a Dowling, and his standing as a Dowling depended on his role in the blood feud. He and his brothers Arthur and Martin were heroes to some members of the clan and lawless outcasts to others. Outlaws or not, now they were needed by the family to protect its members from the Carters. If Gavin came home and struck a blow against the Carters, in spite of their strength, he would become the most feared and respected Dowling in Webster County. That's what he intended to be.

He reached his ranch house without being seen, so far as he could tell. His youngest brother, Everett, came out of the house with a rifle as the lone horseman approached. When Everett saw who it was, he loosed several celebratory shots in the air. These brought their cousin Rachel out of the house to see what was happening—she looked after the place for them, with the understanding that one day she and Martin would marry and build a place of their own. As the eldest of the four brothers, Gavin owned the ranch. This was no big deal because not much private land went with the ranch house—less than three hundred acres. The cattle grazed mainly on the public rangelands—the ground the farmers were chewing up back eastward of them and coming this way. The three elder brothers spent only a couple of months out of each year on the ranch, leaving the care of the cattle to Everett and the care of the house to Rachel.

"Good to see you again, Gavin," Everett said to his brother at the corral.

"I'm pleased to see you with a gun in your hands," Gavin told his youngest brother. "It took you long enough to get some sense. You managed to fuck Rachel yet?"

Everett blushed and glanced around to make sure she was out of earshot. She was. He said, "Don't start that again, Gavin. Let's all be nice to one another."

Gavin's expression turned mean. "You telling me what to do? Is baby brother giving orders now? A kid who can't shoot for shit, living alone in a house with a good-looking woman that he hasn't fucked. There are times when I begin to wonder about you, Ev."

Everett was mad as hell, but the authority of his eldest brother still controlled him. He still felt the need to make explanations. "Rachel's ten years older than me. She helped bring me up as a kid. She's the nearest thing I've had to a mother since I been four. It ain't fair to neither her nor me—not to Martin either—the way you go on at her. She don't like you, and I don't blame her for it, the way you paw at her and say dirty things to her."

"Martin don't give a damn. He ain't ever going to marry her. Even she knows that by now. You're behaving like a dumb shit, Ev. But forget her. She don't count. You going to ride along with me and bag us some Carters?"

"No."

Gavin paused in taking the saddle off his horse and looked his brother straight in the face. "I thought when I saw you carrying that rifle you had growed into a man. You still ain't willing to stand and fight?"

"Not unless I'm attacked."

"And what about when your cousins are gunned down? Don't they count? Or is it only you who matters?"

Ev couldn't help looking guiltily down from his eldest brother's stare. He mumbled, "There just ain't no end to this stupid feuding. It's dumb, that's all."

"All I can say is that it makes me ashamed to have a brother who won't stand shoulder to shoulder with the rest of us to help defend the family. I just don't know what goes on in that head of yours, Ev."

Everett started guiltily. If his brother knew what went on in his head, he'd be in big trouble. If Gavin even *suspected* about him and Emma Carter, there was no knowing where the killing would end.

A few hours after his brother's return, Everett made the excuse that he had to ride out to check on some cattle in a draw. He needed time to himself to think, away from Gavin's powerful influence. Gavin had already begun to set up an attack against the Carters with some other Dowling cousins. One part of Everett wanted to ride in warning to Emma to tell her folk to watch out now that Gavin was here. But he couldn't betray his own flesh and blood by doing such a thing. Once alerted, the Carters would lay in wait for Gavin and surprise him instead of him surprising them. Ev didn't know what to do. He thought of telling Emma and binding her to secrecy, yet he saw how this would be unfair to her—all he would really be doing was unloading some of his problems onto her.

He tried to think as he rode along. When he

couldn't figure anything out, he tried cantering his horse at top speed for a while, slowing down and then thinking again. Nothing worked. He was stuck. Over and over, only one simple solution occurred to him—he and Emma should ride away together, leaving all this hatred behind them, and start a new life someplace far away, like maybe California, where he had heard there was lots of gold for any man willing to dig hard enough to find it. But Emma would never leave her old aunt, who might live to be a hundred. And they couldn't take her with them.

Emma would never forgive him if he rode out with his brother gunning for Carters. Like all other Carters and Dowlings of similar ages, they had been at school together in Bladen. The schoolchildren of the two clans had always mixed with one another, paying no attention to the disagreement and division of the adult world. It was only later that the boys would become involved, dragged in by the menfolk and challenged to prove their worth. Everett wanted no part of this. It wasn't only because of Emma—though that was important; even if he hadn't been in love with her, he would have wanted to avoid this senseless killing between the two families.

His three brothers enjoyed it. There were other Dowlings and some of the Carters like that too. Born to raise hell. They would never let any peace be negotiated. Sooner of later every truce had been broken by a troublemaker, usually just for the hell of it, and some men trying to live in harmony had died as a result of it. Then other decent folk felt their deaths had to be avenged, and soon it was hard to draw a line between the good and the bad, since they were all bent on killing. This happened over and over, sure as fall followed summer, but no one ever seemed to learn from it. Ev didn't fool himself that he was any smarter than anybody else. He knew that if he just once allowed himself to slide into feuding, he'd be as bad as anyone else.

His brother thought he was coming round to his way of thinking when he saw Ev emerging from the ranch house with a rifle in his hands. Ev never wore a sidearm, and he only rarely handled a weapon. In the last few months that had changed. One afternoon he had been riding alone, checking on the cattle, when three Carter boys rode toward him and began shooting at him. He knew all three of them, having gone to school with them, and they knew that Ev had no part in the family bloodletting. All the same, they tried to gun him down and would have succeeded if Ev hadn't been riding his best horse, a big roan stallion that carried him beyond the range of their rifles in a short time.

This incident had brought him to his senses, as his brother Gavin would have said. Ev no longer trusted any Carter man or boy, and let none come near him without having a weapon by him. He realized that it would only be a matter of time before something happened to pitch him headlong into the feud. This made his wish to leave with Emma all the more urgent, but she insisted on staying on to care for her old aunt, refusing to budge, even when he told her she was showing a streak of plain Carter orneriness.

"Give him time," Gavin Dowling snapped. "He'll come around to our way of seeing things."

That shut up the cousin who had made a snide remark about Everett. So far as Gavin was concerned, it was all right for him to make nasty remarks about his youngest brother, but that didn't give every family member the right to do it—at least not in front of Gavin's face, anyway.

Gavin was bullying them, pushing them around, and they were taking it from him. In the end, of course, in order to keep them in awe of him, he would have to give them what they were seeking from him—Carter blood. The male Dowling ranks had been dangerously thinned. It was time to prune some Carter branches, so things would be evened out between them. Gavin intended to give them a bit more than that.

He explained, "It would be no trouble at all for me to ride out and plug some Carter fella chawing his baccy on a corral rail. Then all of us would say we got one of them critters back and feel a bit better for a while. But it wouldn't mean nothing. Now, I didn't go to the trouble of riding all the way back here to Wolf Creek just to blast some old fella who maybe hurt nobody in his whole life but who had the misfortune to be born a Carter. Let me tell you why I came back. I came here to kill the ones who killed our boys. Not just any Carter is good enough for me. I want the ones with Dowling blood on their hands."

This drew a cheer from the men and boys assembled in Gavin's barn. Two jugs of corn liquor were being passed from hand to hand, and fiery words went down well with the fiery liquor. An added thrill was that they all knew Gavin meant what he said—this was no loudmouth boasting.

What they didn't know was that Gavin had left this meeting until the very last moment, not wishing that so many should be aware of his presence at Wolf

Creek until they needed to know. Now they needed to know, because they were coming with him— though he hadn't told them this yet.

"From what I been hearing," Gavin continued after the cheering quieted down, "the first man on our list is Elijah Carter. I went to school with him, and so did some of you. Remember him? He was a low-down skunk then, and he's still a no-good varmint now. Good old Abner had beat the shit out of him in Bladen that day when those other Carter snakes gunned him down. Only reason Elijah survived was he was out cold." Gavin laughed. "Then afterward he takes to strutting around like he was the one who blasted our Dowling boys. He caused the shooting at the graveyard. I'm betting that right now he thinks he's the toughest hombre in Wolf Creek. Well, I got news for him. Bad news. Some of you seen me kick the shit out of him when we was kids at school. Right after I have another swallow of that corn liquor you're passing about, you and me is going to pay a call on Elijah and you're going to see me lay him low in the dirt."

Gavin caught his listeners by surprise. Sure, they expected action from him, but not right there and then, with all of them involved. But no man who wanted to be respected as a man could back out now. They had come to urge Gavin on. They'd sort of forgotten that a man like Gavin didn't need much urging.

"I been told some Carters hired two fiddlers from town to celebrate the birth of a new Carter bastard to Elijah. They're out at his ranch house right now, along with a gathering of kinfolk. I reckon that if all of you was to ride along with me, I might pay my respects to the father. Man to man. One on one. What do you say?"

A few were raring to go, but most were subdued in their enthusiasm. However, no one said no.

"Come on, pass those jugs," Gavin shouted. "Those cheap son-of-a-bitch Carters won't be offering you a drink, you can depend on that."

They rode out in a tight bunch from Gavin's place, thirteen men and boys, each with a handgun and a long gun. Elijah Carter's spread was less than an hour's ride away, on the other side of the creek. As they neared the ranch house, they saw many wagons near it and horses in the corral and tethered in the shade of some trees.

"We're going to be badly outnumbered," one man cautioned Gavin.

"They won't want to do no fighting, not with all their womenfolk and children about," Gavin answered him. "You men hold your fire, and so will they."

They were met by a group of men, numbering close to thirty, many of whom had to hurriedly fetch their rifles from their wagons. Gavin and the others halted their mounts within shouting distance of the house. Then Gavin urged his horse on a few paces until he was clear of the others.

"Y'all know me," he yelled. "I reckon you knew I'd show finally. Well, now you see me. I don't bear ill will to most of you, only to one lying, murdering critter who I hear has been busy breeding more scum like hisself. Now I ain't saying a Carter ain't got a right to be a scum and be left alone. All I'm saying is when he murders decent Dowling folk, then he's a murdering scum. The man I'm talking about is Elijah

Carter, and I'm asking him to come out and face me right now."

By the way the Carters turned their heads, Gavin could tell that Elijah was in their midst. When he didn't step forward immediately, Gavin began laughing and jeering.

"Tell Elijah it ain't no good for him to try to hide," he called. "I can see him plain as day among you. How come you're so shy today, Elijah? Is it because you're a new father? Or is something sceering you? Come out now, Elijah. Don't let everybody see you be afraid. You was a big man down by the graveyard. What you hiding from today?"

It took a while, but at last Elijah stepped out clear in front of the Carter bunch. He held a Colt six-gun in his right hand. Seeing this, Gavin pulled his horse around, and for a moment everyone thought he was going to ride away. But he only returned his horse to the mounted men, swung down out of the saddle, and landed light as a cat upon his feet. He walked the same distance out in front of the Dowlings as Elijah stood before the Carters, stopped, then slowly and carefully drew his Peacemaker. He spun the chambers of the .45 and snapped back the hammer. Then he slowly set off walking at an angle to Elijah.

Elijah started moving forward too, heading at an opposite angle, so that neither man would have his family members directly behind him when the bullets started to fly. It was a well-known fact that, in local gun duels, bystanders got hit as often as the participants themselves. But the assembled Carters and Dowlings had never before seen such a calculated, cold-blooded squaring off in their blood feud, and they didn't like it one bit. This was Gavin's way of doing things—even the Dowlings would have granted that to their worst enemies. There was some excuse when tempers were lost and things happened before anyone rightly thought about the consequences of what they were doing. At times, no killings had been intended, until bad luck intervened. It was admitted now, for instance, that Abner would not have killed Elijah that day in Bladen when Simon Carter and his two nephews happened by and thought Elijah already dead. That was plain bad luck, an understandable mistake. Elijah's boastfulness at the graveyard was stupid and had tragic consequences, yet again it was something a man could understand. But this cold killer stalking Elijah today made things worse in a way they never had been before. Every Carter man who stood in that crowd and looked on saw his own death sentence walking slowly nearer before his eyes.

Elijah did not let the Carters down. He held himself like a man. He fired four times at his opponent, missing each time, before Gavin's first shot brought him down at sixty yards.

Gavin went back to his horse and rode away with his clan, while the Carters carried Elijah to the ranch house on a door. He died four hours later, with his family gathered about the bed. Last thing he asked for was to see once more his newborn child, a healthy boy.

# CHAPTER FIVE

Raider thought about taking a hotel room in Bladen and riding out next day to Wolf Creek. He decided instead to remain in the saddle for three more hours and use the element of surprise in taking Gavin Dowling captive. If he stayed in town overnight, someone might guess what his purpose was and warn Gavin. Raider never ceased to be amazed at how clever the residents of a small town were at guessing a stranger's motives for being among them. And when they were wrong, they usually erred by having too much rather than too little imagination.

When he found Wolf Creek, a cowhand told him that most of the Dowling ranches were on one side of it and most of the Carter spreads on the other. Riding out this way, a man was expected to show where he stood by choosing one side of the creek to ride along.

"I guess then I ought to move over to the Dowling side," Raider said. "You a Carter?"

"Hell, no," the man said. "I'm a hired hand, and come winter I'm gonna ride down to Texas and work along the Pecos. You know that country?"

"I been there. You got some rugged country and wild cows down there."

"You bet, mister, and wild people too—though they ain't no crazier than folks hereabouts. I don't work for any of the Dowling or Carter outfits—they don't hire much outside help—and if I was you, I wouldn't work for none of them either. Specially not as a hired gun."

"What makes you think I might be that?" Raider asked with mild amusement.

"You ain't no cowhand."

"That I'm not. I'm an old friend of Gavin Dowling, come to look him up at home. Know where his place is?"

The cowhand gave him directions, then added casually, "He killed one of the Carters yesterday in a fair fight. I hear he has a fast hand and a calm eye with a gun. You sure you're on good terms with him?"

"We got a real good understanding between us. Thanks for your help. If I see you in town, I'll buy you a drink."

"You best be real careful out here on Wolf Creek if you ever want to make it back to town."

Raider nodded, knowing he hadn't fooled this hard-bitten cowhand for a moment.

The man's directions were sound, and the Pinkerton soon came to the ranch house he had described. Raider kept on the far side of a line of willows on a stream bank so he wouldn't be seen from the house. He dismounted to let his horse drink, then tied it in the shade where there was grass to eat. Reckoning there was less than two hours to sundown, he was not very hopeful of laying eyes on Gavin Dowling today. All the same, he kept a close watch on the house from his place of concealment. An hour or two like this was nothing to Raider—he was prepared to spend a week out here, if he had to, laying in wait for Gavin Dowling.

He wasn't watching long when he heard his horse snicker. Another horse was nearby, but the animal hadn't worked up to a full neigh yet. Raider got to him before he did, keeping him quiet with his fingers on his nostrils. He untied the horse and let it down onto the streambed to keep it out of sight. Raider saw or heard nothing for a few minutes and began to wonder whether it was a false alarm or whether he had been spotted and the other horseman had eased away. Then, where he stood in the clear shallow stream, he saw muddy water flow downstream past him. That had come from the other horse disturbing the bottom as it drank upstream from them. He waited.

In a few minutes, the Pinkerton heard the thud of hooves on the grassland close by. He looked out from the willows and was astounded to see Gavin Dowling ride by him, no more than twenty feet away. Dowling was now clean-shaven, his clothes were washed, and a few days of living under a roof and eating regular meals had made him look like less of a desperado. But a man can't change his face—soap and water won't alter his features. This was the man he was after.

Raider let him pass, then leaped onto his horse's back and spurred the animal hard. The horse burst out of the willows with a crashing sound. Dowling twisted around in his saddle, grabbing for the rifle in his saddle scabbard.

Grateful that Dowling was not wearing his revolver, Raider charged, intending to beat him to the much slower rifle draw. By the time Dowling had the full length of the barrel out of the scabbard, the mounted Pinkerton was almost next to him. He tried to swing the barrel around, but the big man in the black hat was already leaping upon him.

Raider's weight tore Dowling out of the saddle, and the heavy Pinkerton used him to break his fall, crushing the air out of him. Raider quickly tied Dowling's wrists behind his back with rawhide and slapped his face some to get him thinking properly again.

Dowling had recovered by the time Raider had caught the two horses. "You been hired by the Carters?" he asked.

"Don't you know me?" Raider asked in surprise. "I'm the one who came after you from the train."

"What train? I've never even seen a train."

"You seen them well enough to rob them. Now you're going to pay for it. You can call me Raider. I'm a Pinkerton, and I'm taking you down to Wichita to stand trial." He reached into a pocket and took out a wanted sheet. "Here, take a look at your ugly mug."

The Pinkerton held it for him to read, which he did, every word. "This ain't me," he said. "This is my brother Gavin. I'm Everett."

Raider cussed up a storm and threatened to string him up on the nearest willow, but he knew deep down that he had got things wrong. Now that he looked closely, this one was too young to be Gavin.

He finally released him as darkness fell and gave him a message for his brother—that it was time for him to give himself up or to start running again.

Instead of whiskey, Raider had to settle for a long drink of stream water before he found himself a hollow with deep comfortable grass in which to sleep.

Next morning he was gone when Gavin, Everett, and a bunch more Dowlings came looking for him at the stream at first light.

"I didn't expect to find him," Gavin said. "He's a wily bastard, and don't none of you forget that. But there's one thing this Raider fella is leaving out, and that's how us Dowlings is craftier than any Pinkerton."

They all agreed with that, especially the dumber ones.

"This is what we'll do," Gavin said. "I'll go back to the ranch house, and you men quarter the land till you find him. After that, all you need do is bring him within rifle shot of the ranch house and stay back from him so as I get a clear shot."

Everett refused to help, as usual, but the rest of the men took up the search, riding in pairs in case they met up with any Carters. Two of the men did not have far to ride. The others were hardly out of sight when a lone rider approached them—a big man dressed in black, who pulled out a carbine as he neared them and levered a shell into the chamber. This made one of the two Dowlings so nervous that he found a white handkerchief and waved it over his head.

"Gavin wants a truce with you," he shouted to Raider. "He says you and he got to talk."

The Pinkerton said nothing until he came right up to them, nodding in a friendly way like they had no differences between them. "You go tell Gavin that's fine by me."

"He's back at the ranch house. Why not come along with us?"

"I'll wait here."

"Gavin won't want to come here," the other Dowling man said.

"Then he won't get to talk with me like he wants," Raider answered.

"I'm thinking you're going to have to go to him, instead of him to you. Like we told you, he's at the ranch house."

Raider smiled. "If I decide to pay him a visit there, I'll bring along a couple of dozen Carters with me."

"Are you working for them?"

"No," Raider said. "They'll be working for me. Now you go tell Gavin what I just told you. Tell him also that he's to come here alone. I'll be waiting for him. He can bring his guns; that don't concern me. Just don't none of you come in shooting distance of me. I got a nice clear view from here. And don't think of rounding up a posse to hunt me down neither, because if you do, when I see you coming I'll ride over to the Carter side of the creek. Next time I cross back over that creek, I'll bring an army of them with me. You tell that Yankee son of a bitch Gavin that I'm an Arkansas boy. Seems like me and them Carters might have something in common to discuss."

"I knew you was a Southerner," one of the Dowlings said.

"That was right smart of you. Now put that damn-fool handkerchief away and try to remember what I told you to tell Gavin. He's got his truce so we can talk. I'll keep my word on that."

The two men were back in less than an hour.

"Gavin says he's coming straightaway," one said, taking a cloth off an earthenware bowl. "We reckon you must be starving. It's some rice and beans, still warm from the stove."

Raider kept him holding the bowl while he used his left hand to lift a wooden spoonful of the food to the man's mouth. "Eat," Raider said.

The man shook his head. "I ain't hungry."

"Eat."

The man dropped the bowl on the grass and pulled on the reins to back his horse a few steps away.

Raider disgustedly dropped the spoon on the grass. "I reckon there was some varmint pizen added to that mix," he said. "It makes me madder than hell to see good food spoiled that way."

With lightning speed, Raider's right hand dropped to his six-shooter. He whipped it up and snapped off a shot that tore the Dowling man's hat off his head. The gunshot caused his horse to rear, unseating the rider. The Pinkerton jumped off his horse's back and, still holding on to its reins, booted the fallen rider in the gut and on the shoulder. The man howled with pain and rolled away over the grass from the viciously pointed riding boots.

The other Dowling, still mounted, caught Raider's eye on him, although plainly he was not meant too. He was not going to be fooled into drawing his weapon, and sat by, letting his cousin take a beating. The whining, bruised, would-be poisoner limped to his cousin's horse and, helped by him, climbed up behind.

Raider let them go without saying another word. The slimy bastards had been right about one thing— he was starving.

Gavin Dowling rode alone. His Peacemaker was in its holster and his rifle in its saddle scabbard. No one else was in sight on the grassy slight elevation that the Pinkerton had chosen as their meeting place.

Gavin gave Raider a crooked grin and said by way of a greeting, "I hear you have some paper with my face on it."

Raider fetched out a few wanted sheets and cautiously handed them to him. The two men remained in their saddles.

Gavin examined the drawing of his face for some time with evident admiration. He took his time about reading the words also, appearing to be more pleased all the time. "I heard about these," he said, "but I ain't never seen one before. You mind if I hang on to these as souvenirs?"

"If it makes you happy."

"It sure does. This is a real work of art. Look at the way the picture shows my eyes and mouth. Just like in real life. Though it didn't stop you from mistaking my brother for me." He laughed. "You really shook up Everett—it did him a load of good. That boy needs the shit beat out of him about once a day for a year and he'll shape up. You done me a favor."

"He was lucky he wasn't shot," Raider said.

"That would have been a hard way for him to pay for our family resemblance. So you didn't want to bring me in dead? You aiming for one of your Pinkerton courthouse trials, followed by a nice legal hanging maybe, if it all goes your way?"

Raider nodded. "In Wichita."

"What makes you believe you can take me in alive?"

The Pinkerton smiled. "To tell the truth, it ain't my natural inclination to do it that way. But if you was to come quietly, I'd have to do things the courthouse way. If you was to resist arrest, that would be more my style."

"All right, I won't waste your time jawing out here, Raider. This is the deal I want to offer you. We know I came back to Wolf Creek because of family trouble. My cousins need me to protect them from the Carters because of all our menfolk killed in recent times. Why me? Well, some of my cousins is across the state line, and they have to wait for a new sheriff before they can try coming back. Some others we kind of lost touch with for the moment—no one knows where they are. Us Dowlings have some good young fighting men growing here under our nose, but they're not grown men yet, not hardened, and no one wants to lose them so young. And, I'm ashamed to say, some of us is milksops and dreamers who won't help in the fighting. My youngest brother, Ev, is one. He may look like me, but that boy has water, not blood, running in his veins."

"He seemed to me to be normal enough," Raider said. "To me, you look like the one with poison running in his veins."

Gavin's teeth flashed. "Speaking of poison, I hear you didn't like your food."

"Keep talking, and hurry it up."

"Right. It comes down to this. The only real fighting men us Dowlings have at the moment to look out for us is me and my two brothers Martin and Arthur."

"I've heard of them."

"Sure you have. But they ain't where you think they are. You think those boys are robbing trains in Missouri and Kansas, don't you? They've given up that life. Instead they been in San Francisco for months now, earning an honest living as carpenters on all the new houses being built there."

"It's kind of odd for two men who come from the prairies where there's hardly any trees to suddenly become carpenters in a city."

"It surprised the hell out of me when I first heard it," Gavin conceded.

"It surprises me too." Raider didn't bother to tell him that the Pinkertons had evidence that Arthur and Martin had robbed a train in Missouri less than ten days ago.

"Martin and Arthur have been written to, and they wrote back to say they'll be coming back from San Francisco to help out here. Until they arrive, I owe it to my folks to stay here and protect them. You can understand that."

"From what I've heard," Raider said, "you've been making things worse instead of protecting people."

"Then you been talking with Carter supporters. I guess everything depends on a man's point of view. Listen to me careful now. This is the deal I offer you. You stay here with us and help us against the Carters. In exchange for that, when Arthur and Martin arrive, I'll go voluntarily with you for trial in Wichita. What do you say? Will you shake my hand on that?"

"That all you have to offer?" Raider inquired.

"That's the deal, and it's a good one if you want to think about it."

"Not for me it ain't," Raider said. "You're giving me no safeguards that you'll do what you say, and I have reason not to believe what you say about Martin and Arthur."

"They're on their way."

"Maybe," Raider said. "But they ain't become law-abiding men whose word can be depended on."

"So what's your answer, Pinkerton?"

"No deal. Next time you see me, I'm gonna be here to take you in any way you want to go—dead or alive."

Raider found himself a room at R. R. Quickley's Hotel in Bladen, stabled his horse, and bought himself a drink, a shave, and a meal.

"This is good food—best I've eaten in a year or more. I'll have the same again, ma'am."

This time his plate was heaped even higher with roast beef, potatoes, carrots, biscuits, and gravy. "It's on the house," the woman said as she served it. "I just been told you come to bring that sidewinder Gavin Dowling to justice. Eat up, boy. More strength to you."

Raider said, "Thank you kindly, ma'am. I take it you're a Carter supporter."

"I ain't just a supporter. What you see before your eyes is the genuine article, a real full-blood Carter in the flesh."

Raider was curious. "Since this is the only eating house in Bladen, what do the Dowlings do when they're in town, go hungry?"

"No, sir! Their dollar is as good as anyone else's,

far as I'm concerned. Fact is, my daughter Lorna, who does the cooking here, puts an extra special effort on a Dowling's food just to show the critter that Carter women can cook better. Lorna! You come out here right now and meet this gentleman who's come to kill Gavin Dowling. He says you're the finest cook he's come across since he last tasted his mother's home cooking."

Raider was taken aback to find what a pretty daughter this overweight, red-faced woman had. Lorna came out of the kitchen, wiping her hands on a cloth, then releasing her long black hair, which fell loose over her shoulders. Her cool, amused blue eyes surveyed the handsome Pinkerton.

With a very sweet smile, she said, "When you shoot Gavin, aim for his gut so that he dies slowly."

Raider stopped chewing on a piece of beef and stared. He was used to fallen doves swearing and drinking and quarreling, and it concerned him not at all. But being urged to do a killing by two ladies with polite voices and good manners shook him up a bit. "What's so special about Gavin?" he asked.

The mother answered him. "Like I told you, I serve Dowlings food here. Some of them are decent enough folk, though you got to count the spoons after they leave. Some aren't welcome here, and they know it. Martin Dowling killed my husband, Lorna's father. And when Lorna's husband went looking for Martin, Gavin shot and killed him."

"We can't prove any of this," Lorna added. "We were told it by some Dowling women who felt sorry for us. They told us also that most of the Dowlings were against these killings but were too afraid of Martin and Gavin to say anything."

"After that happened—it's been nigh on three years now—Lorna and I were left alone on the ranch. We sold off the stock, the land, and the house, then set ourselves up in business here in Bladen. Business has always been good, but in other ways we've had our ups and downs."

Lorna's blue eyes sparkled cold as ice. "Kill him slow," she said softly.

Raider didn't let this kind of talk spoil his appetite. After he finished the second plate, he ate apple pie and drank strong black coffee. He felt somehow he was being fattened for the kill, in a manner of speaking. After saying goodbye to the two women, he headed down the street for a few drinks. He felt so stuffed with food he couldn't properly enjoy the whiskey, so he decided on a brisk walk to rid himself of the sluggish feeling. It was after three, and the worst of the day's heat was over.

He walked beyond the edge of town and continued in the shade cast by cottonwood trees on a narrow trail. Raider had no idea where the trail led, but following it beat wandering aimlessly. No one was about, and he was considering a nap when he heard a horse behind him. Out of inborn caution, he moved into the trees before the horseman could see him. Content to let the rider pass, Raider looked only after the horse had gone beyond him. He recognized Lorna Carter's long black hair and quickly stepped out and called to her.

She reined in her horse, on which she sat sidesaddle, and looked back at him. "Fancy seeing you here." Then she laughed. "Everyone in town is watching you. I was told you came walking this way. Why were you behind those trees?"

"Force of habit," Raider murmured, feeling a bit silly.

"You men are all the same, always suspicious about being shot in the back or else getting ready to bushwhack someone. You should be more like women."

"You mean we should pull each other's hair and scratch each other's faces?"

"You just don't know any respectable people, Raider. That's caused by the kind of work you do."

"Maybe that's why I do this kind of work."

He assisted her from the saddle to the ground and walked her horse into the trees to tie its reins to a branch. Then they walked together deeper into the cottonwoods, not saying much, though having a good idea of what was in each other's mind. Raider put his arm around her waist, and she snuggled in close to him. They stopped every now and then to kiss, and she didn't resist when he ran his hands over her clothed body.

Raider held her breasts. As he applied pressure, he felt them swell beneath his fingers. Her thighs pressed against him, and he felt his erection grow. She pressed her mound against his stiff dick. He licked the skin of her neck, put his tongue in her ear, and breathed in the fragrant smell of her body.

Her fingers unbuttoned his fly. She held his cock gently and then softly stroked it. His hand crept up her bare leg beneath her dress. He discovered that she was wearing nothing beneath the dress. He stroked and excited her further until she hiked up her dress and wrapped her bare legs around his waist.

Supporting her buttocks in the palms of his hands, he steered his rigid cock into her moist aperture. He buried the head of his prick in her, and then drove its full length into her. She moaned in ecstasy and tightened the grip of her legs around his waist.

Raider walked some more along the path, carrying her on his rigid member. The motion of his walking provided her with extra thrills. Finally he sat on a fallen tree with her straddled on his lap, bouncing up and down, transfixed on his ramrod.

# CHAPTER SIX

Raider had a solid breakfast at the eating house before leaving Bladen next morning to arrest Gavin Dowling. He knew he was riding into trouble and that he had no alternative. Dowling would be expecting him, and there was no way of sneaking up unseen on a man in a prairie ranch house. Every Pinkerton operative found himself from time to time in the position of having to face overwhelming odds. Almost none of them enjoyed it—certainly none of the ones who survived long—although it bothered Raider less than most. He wasn't the sort to lose sleep over what might happen the next day. His experience had taught him that most plans go wrong for unpredictable reasons, and that he who worries least wins most.

He didn't kid himself about the odds, however. No doubt some of the gun-happy cousins would have been summoned in by now to help out. Still, Gavin had called down and killed Elijah Carter in a one-on-one fight. But it was one thing for a gunfighter like Gavin to call down a rancher like Elijah and quite another thing for him to challenge a gun-toting Pinkerton like Raider. Gavin was no fool.

Raider didn't try to figure out all the angles and possibilities. He liked to barge into a situation and think on his feet. This paid off when his opponent buckled under the pressure or made a mistake. It was liable to get Raider clobbered when his adversary didn't scare.

Out on the rangeland, he saw some cowhands working a herd of beeves. When they saw him, they quit working and just stared. Raider had been getting this treatment in town already, and so he knew there was no particular enmity in it—only curiosity about the sort of man who thought he could ride out alone against Gavin Dowling on his home territory.

Looking for information, Raider approached the nearest rider. "Howdy. I see you got them different brands all running together."

"Yeah, these stupid cows don't know Dowling from Carter."

"You keep them separate out on the range?" Raider asked.

"We try to. We don't want no troubles with each other. You can see how we're working peaceably together here. I'm a Dowling, and I don't mind saying I hope you blast that son of a bitch Gavin." The cowhand grinned. "I guess I wouldn't say that in front of his face, though. I don't mind you getting him—just so long as one of these Carter varmints don't do it. Them I'd have to kill."

Raider casually remarked, "I reckon Gavin will have a reception committee for me."

"I reckon."

No more information was forthcoming, so Raider

rode on and the men went back to work separating the cattle. The Pinkerton kept to open country, avoiding draws, clumps of bushes, and anyplace a horseman could lay in wait for him. His horse moved unhurriedly through the tall-grass prairie. It was still a long way to Gavin's ranch house, but Raider was keeping his eyes peeled for trouble. After the cowhands had dropped out of sight behind him, he saw nothing but waving grass and occasional small bunches of cattle.

The bullet sang past his right ear. Another passed close to his shoulder before he located the rifleman's position. The shooter was lying full length on the ground, concealed in the tall grass and weeds. By the time Raider spotted him, he was already levering his carbine. Now he spurred his horse furiously forward, emptying the carbine's seventeen-shot magazine as he went. This was an old cavalry trick Raider had used before—emptying his rapid-fire weapon to force his adversary to lie low while he galloped toward him, intending to trample him with his horse's steel hooves.

So intent was Raider on his murderous mission, he hardly noticed two bullets fired at him from other angles. He couldn't ignore the third—it hit his horse and tumbled them both in the dirt, only twenty yards short of the man Raider intended to run down.

As he fell and hit the grass, Raider clung to his carbine with his right hand. The horse raised its head, tried to struggle upright on its forelegs, and keeled over stone dead.

Raider crawled through the long grass, bullets zinging only inches above him, until he found cover behind his dead mount. Then things swung in his favor. He had four riflemen using him as a target, but now he had the cover of dense horseflesh and they only had grass to hide them. Stems of grass provided rotten protection from a .30-30 bullet.

The Pinkerton managed to hit none of them, and in time he had to conserve his limited ammunition, but he made all four of them crawl more than a half mile on their bellies before they dared to run zigzag and stooping to avoid his accurate fire. They ran another mile before a mounted man brought four horses for them. This gave them the advantage now over the lone dismounted man, but they seemed to have lost their stomach for fighting and rode away in the direction of Gavin Dowling's ranch house.

Raider was damned if he was going to walk back to Bladen. He was damned if he would have Dowling allies in the town laugh at him for returning footsore and weary after a fruitless attempt to bring Gavin in. So he tromped on across the grassland toward Gavin's spread, hoping at least to steal a horse there with the Dowling brand. He realized that what he was doing made no sense, but he was mad as hell and hated more than anything to be laughed at.

That was how his old partner Doc Weatherbee used to get his goat. Weatherbee had settled down to married life, retiring from the Pinkertons—an act which Raider still saw as making him a deserter. He missed Weatherbee in many ways, except for that one thing, the way Weatherbee liked to laugh at him. There were a lot of things Raider was willing to do to avoid being laughed at, and killing a few Dowlings while stealing a horse was one of them. In fact, he was kind of looking forward to it, working up his anticipation with every step through the tall grass.

When he heard the horse behind him and turned around to look, at first he thought he was seeing a mirage. A pretty woman with her hair piled on her head, glinting red in the sun, drove a buggy pulled by a well-cared-for pony. When she came near, Raider noticed that the green of her dress matched the color of her eyes.

"Whoa, hold up, boy!" she shouted, reining in the pony. "You want a lift, stranger, or are you exercising your limbs?"

"Not willingly, ma'am. I'd sure appreciate the ride." He climbed up and sat beside her.

She flicked the reins on the pony's rump, and the buggy moved forward again. She announced matter-of-factly, "My name is Rachel Dowling."

"You a cousin of Gavin's?"

"I sure am," she replied. "Who are you?"

"Name is Raider, ma'am."

"What are you doing in these parts, Mr. Raider?"

"I come to see your cousin."

"Which cousin?" she asked.

"Gavin."

She reined in the pony once more and stopped the buggy. "I'd be obliged if you stepped down, Mr. Raider."

"I'm sorry you insist, ma'am," the Pinkerton said and climbed down from the buggy.

"I'm sure you are, Mr. Raider. No one likes traveling on foot over the prairie in the hot sun."

"Then why did you set me down?"

"'Cause if you're looking for Cousin Gavin, you're either some no-good hell-raising son of a

bitch like he is or you're the law. Either way, you
ain't riding with me."

"I'm a Pinkerton, ma'am."

"Walk any more in the wrong direction and you're
a dead man, Mr. Raider. Dead as that horse back
there. That was your horse, wasn't it?"

Raider nodded. "Why did you pick me up if you
knew I had already been waylaid by somebody?"

She smiled prettily. "Curiosity."

"That kind of curiosity is liable to get a body
killed."

"I'm a Dowling gal, Mr. Raider, and us Dowlings
ain't never been known to steer a wide path from
trouble."

Raider laughed. "So I've heard."

She reached behind her and pulled a blanket from
over a saddle and bridle in the back of the buggy.
Raider recognized them as those from his dead
mount. She asked, "Can I leave these anyplace for
you?"

"Sure. I'd be obliged if you'd leave them with
Gavin and tell him I'll be along for them and him
real soon."

"I take care of the house for the brothers. Maybe
I'll cook something special when you come a-calling." She gave him a mocking smile, flicked the
reins, and drove the buggy away, leaving Raider
standing knee-deep and alone in the waving grass of
the endless prairie.

Raider got some sense into his head, turned around,
and plodded back toward Bladen. This time he saw
no one, and he walked for many hours over the rolling grasslands before arriving in the town at dusk,

thirsty, dust-covered, and exhausted. He drank a gallon of water—a new experience for Raider—ate a meal without hardly saying a word to the two women at the eating house, walked by a half-dozen saloons without even being tempted to go in any of them, and finally flopped down on his hotel bed.

He got his gunbelt and boots off but was too tired to take off his clothes. He lay like a felled tree trunk on the bed and soon was snoring like a buzz saw. It was some time before the banging on the door roused him. He groped around for his gun and snapped back the hammer.

Aiming the barrel at the door, he roared, "Is this hotel on fire? If it ain't and you woke me up, you miserable son of a bitch, I'm gonna drill a hole between your eyes and I don't care if I swing for it."

From the other side of the door, he heard a girlish giggle that he recognized. He sighed and eased down the hammer on his thumbnail. When he opened the door, Lorna Carter rushed at him and embraced him tightly.

"I was so worried," she gasped. "You were gone all day without any message. Then you ate your meal—which I made specially for you—without a smile or even a glance at me. What could you expect me to feel? How could you do this to me?"

"Lorna, I'm tired, very tired."

"That's no excuse." She pouted. "You got what you wanted. Now you don't care for me anymore."

Raider fell back on the bed. "Sweetheart, if you can manage to get these clothes off me and somehow keep me from falling asleep, I'll do my best to show you my affection."

Lorna nodded in a businesslike way. "Very well," she said. "We'll start with the pants."

At dawn next day, Raider went to see the stable owner about renting a horse and saddle, for he intended to make Gavin Dowling replace his dead horse and return that saddle. The two extra mounts Raider had picked up at the train robbery had been sold by him at Latrobe. The stable owner claimed that the saddle was worth $65 and the horse $35, for a total of $100. Raider knew he could easily have beaten him down to $80, but this was the only stable in town, and he needed another horse and saddle right away.

"Put it on my bill," Raider said.

The stable owner stuck out his hand. "Cash."

Raider dug deep in his pocket and gave him five twenty-dollar gold pieces. "I need a receipt," he said.

"I can't write," the stable owner said, reaching for the coins.

Raider's fist closed around the gold. "Find someone who can."

Like the proverbial Scotsman, Allan Pinkerton was tightfisted about expenses. This irked Raider, because he knew that the client, not Pinkerton, had to make good all the expenses incurred. There was never a word about Raider's lucky escapes from being shot—only complaints about the number of horses he had had shot out from under him. More than any other Pinkerton operative. Nothing was said about the more dangerous assignments he was given, only about his reckless disregard for property. The Chicago head office wanted receipts, reports, itineraries, estimates. . . . They expected only very little from Raider, and he always made sure they got less.

When the stable owner's young son had written a receipt and the gold changed hands, Raider selected another horse and saddle. He set out on the ride to Wolf Creek with a pair of sore feet to remind him of the previous day's humiliation.

Today was going to be different. Raider wasn't sure in what way it was going to be different—only that it was going to be. This time he took a slightly different route to Wolf Creek, hoping to fool any riflemen waiting in ambush. He saw a few distant riders in the area where most of the cattle were grazing, and he kept too far away from them to be recognized. After that it was just miles of empty rangeland. The going was slower through the tall grass because he was keeping his horse away from the beaten-down trails. Finally he came in sight of the ranch house. He quickly dismounted and tied his horse out of sight in a clump of willows by a waterhole.

Yesterday he had made the Dowlings crawl on their bellies through the grass. Now it was his turn. That ranch house was a long way off, and that was a lot of grass and a lot of crawling—but there was no other way for him to get close to the house unseen. Raider could only hope that after all his effort, Gavin would be there when he arrived. He left his hat behind with his horse, but took his carbine. A man with a height of six feet and two inches and a bone and muscle weight of 200 pounds has a lot of advantages in life—however, one of them is not crawling through grass unseen. A short temper is not much of a help either. Even if Raider couldn't be seen, much of the time he could have been heard cursing stinging leaves, thorny scrub, four stinging bees, and a truculent snake.

"Why the hell ain't you out there along with everyone else, looking for this Pinkerton critter who means us nothing but harm?" Gavin Dowling shouted at his brother Everett in the ranch house kitchen. "If I can't ask my own brother—my own flesh and blood —to look out for me in a time of danger, how can I ask first cousins, uncles, nephews, second cousins to do what my own brother won't do? Fortunately, I don't have to ask. Fortunately, they know their duty to family—and don't allow themselves to get put off by one pantywaist like you."

Everett stared out the window, sitting at the table with a mug of coffee in his right hand. "I ain't killing no Pinkerton just because you're too lazy and no-good to stay home and ranch. Who does the work around here? I do—and I don't even own the damn place. I do all the work while you and Martin and Arthur rob trains and blow the money in cow towns on poker, booze, and loose women." He broke off hurriedly, with a glance at Rachel.

She smiled bitterly. "You don't have to be careful about what you say 'cause of me, Ev. I know what Martin does for relaxation. Ain't a lot of fun being engaged to a man who prefers whores and saloons to a family and home."

"You know what I said to that Pinkerton after he dang near crushed me to death, knocking me off my horse?" Everett was incensed. "He accused me of being a train robber, and I told him I've never even seen a train! Now I been thinking about that. I think it's about time I seen one."

Gavin's face brightened. "Glad to hear it, Ev. I'll take you with me on my next job."

"I don't want to rob one," Everett yelled. "I want to travel in one as a passenger, like a civilized person."

Gavin stared at him in amazement. "Where you going?"

"Where I'd be going is not the thing that counts, Gavin. What matters is feeling like a regular person just once in my life. Don't you ever wonder what it would be like without Carters trying to shoot you in the back, without the law chasing you for something you done?"

"No."

Ev smiled. "That figures. Well, *I* wonder what it would be like. The Carters have no good cause to want to kill me, except to get at you through me. The law has no cause to come after me, 'cause I ain't done nothing. That's my trouble—I ain't done nothing."

Gavin nodded in agreement. "You ride out with me, Ev, and we'll fix that."

Rachel put in sharply, "Don't you go nowhere with him, Ev. He'd ride off and leave you bleeding in the dirt and it wouldn't bother him none."

"You're getting sour and mean, Rachel," Gavin said. "What you need is some good loving to make you see the brighter side of life. If the pantywaist here can't give it to you, maybe I will. Maybe tonight. You'll go around tomorrow with a smile on your face, instead of that lonesome miserable look you have now."

"Don't start me on again!" Rachel screeched.

Everett said in a quiet voice, "Leave her alone."

"I warned you before, boy," Gavin snarled, "don't talk back to me. Maybe when I sort out some of these other troubles, I'll take off some time to straighten you out."

"You'd best find someone else to work this ranch for you before you do," Ev threatened.

"And to cook and clean and wash," Rachel added in.

These were not things Gaving wanted to talk or think about. "I have to listen to you two whine while a bounty-hunting Pinkerton is stalking me and the Carters are putting theirselves an army together to assassinate me."

"I been hearing that," Rachel put in. "They were saying in Bladen yesterday that if the Carters can kill you now, Arthur and Martin won't dare return to Wolf Creek, and if they do, the Carters will be ready for them."

"With us three gone," Gavin mused, "there'd be no holding back the Carter scum. They'd force us off the rangeland, and we'd have to sell out cheap to them."

"The farmers are going to do that to us in a few years anyway," Everett said.

"Not while I'm drawing breath," Gavin said. "We'll worry about them when they show their faces. I got troubles nearer at hand than dirt-turning farmers."

Gavin Dowling never said a truer thing. As he spoke, sitting on a kitchen chair on the opposite side of the table from Ev, facing the door that led outside, the big Pinkerton came headlong through the open window behind him and landed on Gavin's back in a pounce that would have done any mountain lion proud.

The chair on which Gavin sat was shattered, and the weight of the two men hitting against its side overturned the long pine table onto Ev, who ended up beneath it on the floor. Raider beat Gavin over the head and shoulders with a broken-off chair leg until he grew docile. Everett was struggling out from beneath the table. The Pinkerton looked up to see Rachel coming at him with a carving knife. She faltered under his steady gaze and finally stopped, putting the knife aside on a dresser.

"Don't hurt Everett," she said.

Raider nodded his agreement.

She pointed at Gavin, sitting groggily on the floor, holding his head. "You can give him an extra one for me."

Raider obliged, cutting Gavin's left ear with a smart crack of the chair leg.

Rachel smiled. "But don't kill him."

"The hangman in Wichita will do that," Raider told her. He turned to Ev, who was now on his feet. "Boy, reach out that window and bring my carbine in from where I left it leaning on the wall. You'll keep in mind while you're doing it that I have a .44 on my right hip."

Ev kept it in mind, holding the carbine by the barrel and passing it to the Pinkerton butt first. Raider had taken Gavin's .45 Peacemaker and tucked it into his own gunbelt, and now was tying Gavin's wrists behind his back with a length of rope.

"Boy," he said to Everett, "you have some jobs to do. First, you ride out to your cousins laying in wait for me, and tell them what happened, and promise them I'll kill every one of them that comes in carbine range of this ranch house. Then go to the willows by the waterhole and bring me my horse and hat. You be careful with that hat or I'll skin you alive. Bring them back here. Then I want you to put the saddle this fine lady brought here for me yesterday and put it on a good horse of yours to replace the one of mine you people shot."

"Why the hell should I do that for you?" Ev sneered in a sudden change of his usual mild personality.

"For two reasons," the Pinkerton told him. "First reason is that I'm going to shoot your cousins anyway when they come in carbine range, so maybe if you warned them in advance, fewer will die. I don't really care one way or the other. As for my hat, the saddle, and the extra horse, it's like this. If I don't have my hat, I'll use Gavin's and he can ride bareheaded in the sun. And if I don't get my saddle back and a replacement horse, Gavin won't have nothing to ride on, so he'll have to trot along behind my horse on a length of rope with a noose around his neck. Any other questions on your mind?"

"No."

"Get moving then. You," he said to Rachel, "promised to cook me something special next time I came a-calling. Well, here I am, hungry and waiting. Better get that stove fired up."

# CHAPTER SEVEN

"I'm telling you that Ev Dowling rode up to his cousins and warned them to stay away from the ranch house. Some of our cattle had wandered over that way—they were on Ev's land—and he told us not to drive them off in case the Pinkerton shoots us. Seems like he's taken Gavin prisoner and is holed up in the ranch house. Only other person inside is Rachel."

"You can't believe what them lying devil's spawn tells you," old Toss Carter said to his nephew Hugh.

"I sat beside Ev in the schoolhouse," Hugh protested. "I don't bear him no grudge, and he none to me. He didn't have to say a word to me, except out of friendliness."

"Or maybe he was setting a trap for you—or us, more likely." Toss opened his toothless mouth to cackle, and his splintered fingernails scratched the white stubble on his bony jaw."Gavin forced him to do it 'cause he's heard I'm rounding up the men to nail his hide to a barn door while we've got the chance. If either or both of his murdering brothers show, there'll be few men willing to raise a hand against them. This is our chance. We've got to take it. Push them Dowlings down far enough now, they'll never rise again."

Hugh shrugged. "I don't know. Why don't you ride over and see for yourself? Gavin's men are just standing around and riding hither and yon, keeping their asses out of range. They ain't in no mood to pick a fight with you. Last thing they need right now is a mob of us Carters looking for blood."

Toss winked a bloodshot eye. "That's just my thinking. So, supposing this ain't a Dowling trick, that that Pinkerton is for real. A hundred folks have seen him in Bladen."

"He came back to town barefoot and dragging his ass last night after Gavin whupped him," another Carter said. "Whole place was laughing at him behind his back."

"Same folk may be laughing at Gavin tonight," Toss observed. "Being a Pinkerton, this Raider fella ain't going to string the buzzard up, like any normal God-fearing citizen would. He'll be set on bringing Gavin to some highfalutin courthouse trial, where some judge and a jury of city slickers will say tut-tut to Gavin, make him promise to be good, and let him go after six months. Now I don't think that's a fitting way to treat a weasel once he's got one of his legs caught in a trap. I think you should put the varmint out of his pain soon as possible. And that's what I aim to do with Gavin."

Toss went on, "This Pinkerton, from what I been hearing of him, is raw and mean and don't fear nothing this side of the Gates of Hell. He ain't going to let a bunch of ranchers keep him holed up in that house. If he has to, he's going to bring Gavin out over their dead bodies. And you and me know, there ain't one of them Dowlings there who is worth a fuck in a fight, except Gavin. That's why we got to get rid of him."

Hugh was no fool. "If this Raider is a hard man, as well as killing off the Dowlings, he'll kill us off if we mess with him."

"Difference will be," Toss put in, "he's expecting the Dowlings. We'll be a surprise."

"I say we leave well enough alone," one Carter announced. "This Pinkerton is taking care of him for us."

Hugh said, "I agree."

Toss scowled. "Gavin killed Elijah. He was my nephew, same as you, Hugh. If Gavin had killed you, would you be satisfied to know as you died that I would leave justice to the hand of some stranger? Never! Gavin spilled our blood, and it's us that have to make him pay in blood for what he done. For all we know, some judge somewheres, like I said before, will give him a short spell in jail or he'll get some politician's pardon. I want Gavin Dowling beneath the sod, not behind bars."

Raider got his hat back in good shape, and he was much relieved. He watched through the window while Ev Dowling put the two horses in a small corral with some shade, where there was a water trough and a mound of feed. Ev put the two saddles and bridles on the top rail.

"That'll do fine," the Pinkerton called to him out the window. "You best be gone, buckaroo, and keep yourself and your cousins at a distance unless you want the buzzards feeding off you."

"You want me to tell them in Bladen you'll be coming there?" Ev inquired with mock innocence.

Raider laughed. "I can see that some of you dumb shits are planning on messing with me. Before you do, be sure to say your prayers and say goodbye to your loved ones."

Without knowing it, Raider had touched a tender spot in Ev's defenses. Ev immediately thought of Emma and how he wanted to take a train with her far away from Wolf Creek. She had once joked that if they tried it, maybe one of his brothers would chance to stop the train in order to rob it, spot them, and force them to return. Ev had this awful feeling he was foredoomed never to see a train, never to escape from Wolf Creek. Here he was now, letting himself be drawn into his brother's escapades, trying to out-smart a Pinkerton who was every bit as cagey and tough as Gavin. Emma was all that mattered now to him. If Gavin knew about his feelings for her, Gavin would kill him. He had to choose between her and Gavin. Trying to rescue Gavin from this Pinkerton was choosing him over her. Yet he couldn't just sit by and see his brother led away, even if Gavin deserved it. Right or wrong, he had to stick by his own. Tormented and confused, Ev slowly mounted his horse and let it walk out onto the open grassland toward the far-off figures of his cousins, who now had the house surrounded.

Rachel left her stove repeatedly to watch him go. She said, "It's kind of surprising how he turned out all right and the other three are all serpents."

Gavin, alert again, spat on her clean floor but said nothing.

Raider looked out at the hot midday sun beaming down from a cloudless sky. He was in no hurry, easy and relaxed. "That food sure smells good," he said. "Chicken, ain't it?"

"Chicken and dumplings and fresh green peas," Rachel said.

"You goddamn traitor!" Gavin yelled at her. "Why are you feeding him?"

Raider said to him, "She's cooking for you as well as me. My advice to you is enjoy it while you can. Where you're going, if they don't hang you, it'll be twelve or fifteen years before you taste home cooking again."

They passed the whole afternoon in the kitchen without the Pinkerton giving them any idea of what he intended to do. He seemed content to stay where he was and even dozed off in a chair after his big feed of chicken and dumplings—but one eye opened whenever either of them moved. Gavin sat quietly, hands bound behind him, waiting and watching for just one mistake. Raider's nonchalance and Gavin's tenseness and her lack of knowledge about what was going to happen next got on Rachel's nerves, and she busied herself around the kitchen. When all her chores were done, since she was not allowed to leave, she polished knives, forks, and spoons, mopped the floor a second time, blacked the stove, glued some loose recipes into a notebook, and practically went out of her mind.

She knew the cool, calm Pinkerton was enjoying her discomfiture, especially after the way she had treated him the previous day, making him walk. Every now and then she met his eye. What really annoyed her was that she couldn't help liking him. He was her kind of man—handsome, big, and rough. She only hoped he couldn't guess what was going on in her mind.

When it got dusk, he had her place oil lamps in some of the windows. Then they went back to sitting. Gradually it grew dark. Suddenly the Pinkerton was on his feet. Carbine in his left hand, he used his right to lift Gavin out of the chair by one armpit and propel him out the door in front of him.

"Rachel, you don't touch those lamps," Raider ordered. "Follow us out into the dark."

He waited a spell by the corral until his eyes were accustomed to the dark. Then, keeping Gavin and Rachel where he could see them, he caught and saddled both horses. He helped Gavin onto one, binding his wrists before him to the saddle horn. Next he tied a lariat from the bridle of Gavin's horse to the back of his saddle.

"We're ready to move out," he said to Rachel. "You go back in the house and sit quiet for a few hours. Don't move those lamps. If you do, it will be taken as a signal that something is happening. Leave them like they are and maybe they'll think we're still in the house. You understand me, Rachel? You don't want Ev to be hurt. I know you feel like a mother to that boy. Neither you nor me wants him hurt. So don't signal him by moving those lamps."

She nodded.

Raider could tell by Gavin's disgruntled grunt that she would abide by what he said.

•  •  •

Horses don't bump into things in the dark. When let alone to do so, they find their way safely enough. The constellations of stars in the clear night sky provided low-level illumination—in fact, more than Raider would have wished for. Keeping the North Star at his back, Raider headed due south for Bladen and, beyond that, the Kansas state line and, farther still, the railroad. Gavin could figure that much. What he couldn't figure was how Raider intended to break out of the encirclement of his cousins and stay alive himself to bring his prisoner in. He sat quietly on his horse, a rope's length behind Raider's animal, offering no resistance until he saw his opportunity.

There was a good possibility the Pinkerton might pick up an escort of sheriff's deputies at Bladen to go with them as far as the state line, or the Pinkerton might dump him in the Bladen jail to be collected later by federal marshals. Once they were outside of Wolf Creek, the balance began to swing in the Pinkerton's favor, there was no doubt about that. That only went to fortify one thing in Gavin's mind— come what may, he and this Pinkerton were not leaving Wolf Creek.

Raider rode the fresh horse Ev had provided. Out of force of habit and keeping to ground it knew, this horse stuck to the trail beaten through the years over the ranchlands and ranges toward Bladen. Gavin knew this. He was hoping Raider didn't. The Dowling cousins couldn't miss them now, and soon as he saw one, Gavin intended to raise a holler. This Pinkerton dude was slick and he was tough, but he was in Dowling country. Gavin grinned. Maybe they wouldn't kill him—only send him back to town on foot for a second time in two days. To a man like

Raider, that would be worse than killing him, a blow like that to his pride.

They moved quietly on under the stars. It seemed for a while that they were going to walk through the encircling Dowlings without being seen or heard. Suddenly they heard a yell, off to one side in the darkness.

"It's me! Gavin!" the Pinkerton's captive shouted. "He's taking me in, lads."

A series of shouts sounded as the Dowlings alerted their sentinels.

"Here," Gavin called to them. "Over this way."

Raider ignored everything, neither quickening nor slackening his horse's pace.

A small group of horsemen came in their direction, the horses stumbling at times in the darkness. Gavin guided them with shouts. When they sounded very close, the Pinkerton pulled on the lariat to Gavin's horse, drawing it in so that both horses walked side by side. Then Raider drew his Remington .44 and fired two shots at the approaching riders. They fired wildly back at the two spurts of flame.

"Quit firing, you dumb bastards!" Gavin screamed. "You nearly hit me. He's hiding behind me, wanting you to kill me for him."

Raider replaced the two spent cartridges by feel and kept the two horses moving forward side by side. He still hadn't said a word to his prisoner.

"Slow him down and we'll surround you," a Dowling called.

Gavin rolled out of the saddle and was dragged along, his boots trailing over the grass, by his two wrists tied to the saddle horn. Feeling the pull, his horse tried to stop, but Raider forced the animal to keep up its pace and haul its burden.

"This rope is cutting my fucking hands off," Gavin complained.

Raider finally spoke. "Just so long as those two hands are where I tied them, I don't much care if you're still attached to them." He quickened the pace of the horses.

Gavin got the message real fast. He ran alongside his horse, put a foot in one stirrup, and swung his other leg over the horse's back. When he was back in the saddle again, he began cursing his useless cousins who were no better than a lot of low things that he listed by name.

The Dowlings followed them through the night, relying on Gavin's shouts for their bearings. Twice more, Raider fired on moving shadowy forms. Gavin yelled at them not to fire back, telling them they would get an opportunity and to bide their time. They rode for some time, making slow progress by starlight, with the bunch of horsemen a couple of hundred yards behind them. Raider kept Gavin close by him but made no attempt to quiet him.

They were down by Wolf Creek, where the trail ran alongside the creek, when they saw a lantern ahead. There were no houses along this stretch, and at first Raider assumed it was a cowhand's overnight camp. He set out to make a wide detour but then noticed that the lamp was set on a wagon overturned on its side. A woman stepped into the area of light, clasping her hands and taking nervous steps back and forth.

Raider approached closer, noting that Gavin was growing very uneasy. The Pinkerton was wondering if this was some kind of Dowling trap for him. If it was, Gavin didn't seem too happy about it.

"Know her?" Raider asked.

"I ain't sure. Let me get a good look at her face." As he said this, the woman turned so that the lamp illuminated her features. "It's that woman from Omaha who married a Carter. He got hisself killed by one of us. She's a widow woman looking for revenge. Don't go near her!"

Raider had a hard choice to make. A man like him didn't turn his back on a lone woman who needed help. Yet he believed Gavin that she was one of the Carters and that this looked suspicious. He might have detoured around her if it hadn't been for the Dowling riders behind. He didn't know what they would do, but he couldn't leave her alone to take her chances with them.

He rode toward her, paying out the length of rope so that Gavin was behind him again. He did this so that she wouldn't be frightened by seeing Gavin when he rode into the lamplight.

"My horse bolted," she called to him. "I don't know what to do here alone. Who are you?"

"A Pinkerton, ma'am, taking a prisoner in. I'd put you up behind me on my horse and take you to Bladen, 'cept we have some Dowling horsemen back there who'll be doing some shooting before long. Gavin is my prisoner."

She peered out toward the edge of the circle of light where she could see a man on a horse. "Is that Gavin?" she asked.

"It surely is," Raider answered her.

She responded by running as hard as she could into the darkness.

Raider called after her, "It's all right. His hands are tied and he can't come after you."

Two men stood up from behind the cover of the overturned wagon. Both had rifles.

"Don't you move," one was saying to Raider, whose right hand was already hauling his long-barrel revolver from its holster.

They saw him draw and both tried to shoot him. They were slow and clumsy in comparison to him. They didn't handle their weapons as if they were parts of themselves. The Pinkerton squeezed the trigger before his gun barrel reached the line of fire, and the edge of his left hand fanned back the hammer in two rapid shots.

The ambushers died a second apart from one another. The first bullet stove in the forehead of one, and the second bullet tore off the side of the other man's head. Neither had managed to fire their weapons.

In that terrible instant of silence that followed, Raider tried to move his horse out of the lamplight. He almost made it before a volley of shots came at him from the other side of the creek. These weren't Dowling bullets, he had time to realize that, before he felt a searing pain in his left leg.

The agony welled up inside his body. He felt himself about to fall from the saddle or lose consciousness—he wasn't sure which—and only an effort of will kept him going. He made it to Gavin, pulled his bowie, and cut through his bonds. Gavin snatched his own revolver from Raider's belt. Raider slumped against him as he fell out of the saddle.

Bullets whistled and whined around them as the two men tumbled out of their saddles between the horses. Gavin shot out the lamp and then pulled Raider to the cover of the wagon. They were safe there from the shots across the creek. Raider was bleeding badly. As he grew more weak and light-headed from loss of blood, the pain eased. He slowly lost consciousness.

Meanwhile the Dowling riders were returning Carter fire. The shooting didn't amount to much, but it lasted a long while and prevented the Carters from crossing Wolf Creek to collect their dead or finish off their enemies.

# CHAPTER EIGHT

Raider woke up in bed. The pain in his left leg reminded him of what had happened. Everett Dowling walked into the room, and when he saw Raider awake and stirring he called Rachel. They both made him comfortable. Rachel changed the dressing on his leg.

"I took the bullet out," she said. "You started bleeding bad again, but I managed to stop it. It's a flesh wound—the bone wasn't touched. So long as infection don't set in, you'll be all right. This wound looks clean. I guess it ain't the first time you been shot, judging by the scars I seen on your body." She blushed, having made this admission.

Raider realized he was wearing nothing but a nightshirt. "Where's my gun?" he asked.

"Gavin's got it."

"I want to thank you for caring for me," Raider said sincerely. "Are you a nurse?"

"No, but I've had some experience fixing wounds all along Wolf Creek," she said bitterly. "Most of us women do, when we ain't burying the men."

"Things have been bad, I know."

"And they ain't getting better," she said. "Us women fix the men and then they go out and get shot again. It's a fool's game. If I'd any sense, I'd get far from here while I still could. How're you feeling? You hungry?"

"I was wondering if maybe there was some of that chicken and dumplings left," Raider said.

"How could there be? You and Gavin finished it all. There's pork out on the stove. I'll bring you in some. Going to be a couple of days before you leave that bed, and another week before you ride a horse again, all going well."

She underestimated Raider. In a couple of hours he was in his clothes and hobbling about with the aid of a cane he found in a corner. He could hide the pain that walking caused him; what he couldn't hide was his pallor and weakness. The loss of blood had taken its toll. He ate ravenously and drank mugs of spring water to build up his blood supply again. All the same, waves of dizziness swept over him without warning, and he had to sit quickly or fall.

Gavin returned in the early afternoon, apparently in very good humor. "How are they treating you, Raider? Don't put up with any nonsense from them. You're our guest. If you want something, all you have to do is ask for it."

"I want my gun."

Gavin laughed. "Well, I said you could ask for anything you wanted. I didn't say you'd get it. I have your revolver and your carbine, along with the horses and saddles. We used one horse to pull you back on that wagon the Carters left. Remember that?"

Raider nodded.

"I'm going to make you that offer I made before," Gavin went on. "You stay with me and help fight off the Carters until my brothers arrive, then I'll go peaceably with you to stand trial."

"You're holding the gun," Raider said. "Why make an offer?"

"You saw who I have to help me fight the Carters. They couldn't even stop you taking me away as your prisoner. I don't know how that might have ended if it wasn't for the Carters interrupting. Chances are you'd have wiped out the whole dang lot of them. All our good Dowling fighters are dead, like Abner, or are away somewhere else, like my brothers. The Carters are going to make a move on us real soon. I need a man who can shoot like you. The way you nailed those two behind the wagon—I've never seen nothing so fast and accurate as that. And I know you can use that carbine from the way you took out my two pards back at that train we tried to rob."

"Those two weren't Dowlings?"

"Hell, no. I don't hold their deaths against you. That was fine shooting."

Raider thought about it for a moment. "I turned your offer down before because I wasn't being offered any assurance you would keep your word and come along with me when the time came. I guess you're telling me now that I've no choice but to take your word on it."

Gavin grinned his assent.

"What makes you so sure I'll keep my part of the agreement?" Raider asked. "Like with fighting off the Carters?"

Gavin's grin got wider. He left the room for a

moment and returned with Raider's gunbelt and carbine, which he placed beside him. His face turned serious. "The Carters are being stirred up by an old coot name of Toss. He was born down there in South Carolina and fought for the Confederates. Sherman's men or Grant's—I don't recall which—shot them up and burned their homes and then they got cheated out of their land after the war was over. His mind is still back in them bad old days, and he still has scores to settle. He's plain loco, and that's the truth of it. Anyway, he's got two favorite nephews. I shot one of them—Elijah. You killed the other—Hugh. So you and me has a lot in common, Raider, so far as old Toss Carter is concerned." Gavin's grin returned. "Fact is, I heard today that there's only one man in Webster County that the Carters hate more than me."

Raider dipped a clean square of cloth in some light oil and began cleaning his guns.

"Can't you stay with someone in town awhile or with one of your cousins?" Emma Carter asked.

Everett Dowling looked at her hard. "You heard them planning an attack on our place?"

Emma squirmed. "I can't be disloyal to my folks, Ev. I don't want you hurt is all."

Ev thought about this for a time, while Emma fretted. Finally he said, "This stuff is going to tear us apart, Emma, if we let it. We have to stand together against it. This is what we'll do. You tell me what you heard—and don't count on it as betraying your folks, 'cause I ain't going to pass the information along to Gavin. I'll just tell the Pinkerton what he needs to know to stop the fighting. Gavin ain't exactly afeared of him, but he'll do what the Pinkerton says since he respects him."

"No!" Emma cried vehemently. "That low yella-bellied traitor to the Cause!"

"What cause?"

"The Cause! The South! That man's a Southerner! He's from Arkansas, and he's bedded in with you Yankee Dowlings. He's a traitor!"

Ev started laughing. "What's come over you, Emma, talking like that? You been listening to your Uncle Toss?"

She dropped her eyes. "Well, it's true."

"No, it ain't true. You and me weren't even born till after the War Between the States. Raider ain't more than ten years older than us. Oldest he could have been at the end of the fighting was six, maybe seven. You think he might have been a drummer boy with Robert E. Lee?"

Emma giggled. "That kind of joke would get you killed in our house."

"In mine, too, most likely. But I wouldn't dare make jokes about Southerners with Raider around. He's a bit of a Rebel."

"I thought you said he wasn't."

"I'm afraid he is," Ev said. "That's why Gavin don't want him near any of you folks. You all think the same."

"That's why Uncle Toss and the others hate this Pinkerton so much. Ev, they're coming after him. They're going to burn the ranch house with y'all in it and stick you like rats if you try to come out."

"When?"

"Tonight, I think."

"I'll fix it with Raider so no one gets hurt. You'll see."

Emma sighed. "I feel guilty and relieved, both at the same time, now I've told you."

"It ain't easy, Emma. But soon, real soon, you and me is going to be far away from here."

She let him caress her where they lay on the soft grass in the willows by Wolf Creek.


Ev waited until Gavin went to the barn to check on some things. He glanced at Rachel, who nodded to him, and then he said to Raider, "The Carters are gonna try to burn us up inside this house, maybe tonight."

Raider's right eyebrow rose a quarter inch. "Who says?"

"Some people told me. They didn't want to see me hurt."

"People?" Raider inquired.

"Yeah, people."

Raider picked up his cane in his left hand, rose out of his chair, and hobbled across the kitchen to Ev, who stood nervously by the stove. The Pinkerton stood in front of him for a moment, then raised the cane and swung it viciously down toward Ev's head. Ev took some fast steps out of the way. Raider checked the cane's swing and tossed it between Ev's feet, tripping him and bringing him to the floor. Three limping steps brought the Pinkerton towering over the fallen youth. Using only his left hand, Raider picked Ev up by the shirtfront until his feet were lifted off the floor. He ignored Rachel screaming at him and wordlessly threw Ev against the wall.

The youth hit the rough-hewn planks with his

back and collapsed in a heap on the floorboards. Rachel was still screaming loud enough to raise the dead. Raider picked him up left-handed again by the shirtfront.

"You can't fool an old hand like me, kid," the Pinkerton ground out. "You got some underhand shit going—if the lady will pardon my language. I aim to know what it is before I act on your information. I'm not a curious sort, only when I need to know. You're holding something back on me. Think I don't notice you wait till Gavin is gone before you tell me some 'people' gave you information? He'd tear your hair out by the roots until he found out who you'd been talking with. Maybe you're giving these 'people' information about us, too, eh? A goddamn serpent in our midst!"

He raised Ev in his left hand once more, preparatory to throwing him against the wall, when Rachel laid the blade of a carving knife across his throat. Raider froze, holding Ev suspended in midair.

"I mean it, Raider," she sobbed. "You hurt that boy, I swear to God I'll open your throat."

"Listen, careful, Rachel," the Pinkerton said in a cold, flat voice. "My right hand is four inches from the handle of my shooting iron. You start slicing anytime you like, but I guarantee you ain't going to have much of a scratch made on my throat by the time a hot .44 tears through you from point-blank range."

The standoff lasted a few more seconds.

"So help me God," Rachel cried out, "I'll do it! I'll do it!" The knife blade trembled in her hand against Raider's windpipe.

Ev, his feet still off the floor, looked from one to the other, bug-eyed with fright.

Raider said to him in an easy way, like they were in some saloon, "You see the trouble with women, Ev? You can explain something to them, and if they don't want to understand it, they won't."

He set Ev down gently on his feet and released the grip on his shirtfront.

The blade was lifted off Raider's throat.

"Hand me my cane, kid," Raider said to Ev, and he used it to hobble back to his chair, saying, "I reckon that with time I'm gonna make a sweet old man. People will call me Pops. I'll drill the rats."

Rachel and Ev watched him settle in the chair. Rachel had a look on her face that showed she couldn't quite believe what she had just done.

"Ev, those farmers ten miles east that you were telling me about," Raider began in an easy tone that seemed to cancel everything that had gone before.

Rachel and Everett just stood and stared, bewildered by this sudden change of subject. Raider spelled out what he had in mind.

"Better get yourself a bunch of men and be back by dusk," Raider told him at the end. "And tell those men if they hurt someone they don't have to, they answer to me. You got money?"

"No," Everett said.

"Tomorrow you can drive over a few steers."

Everett left in a hurry.

Once they were alone, Rachel started giggling.

Raider looked at her grumpily, "What's so funny?"

"You saying you could shoot me," she said.

"I don't reckon I could," he admitted.

"I'd have cut your throat, though. I meant it."

"Oh, I can believe that," he said.

Gavin came through the door. He looked from one to the other of them with a grin. "Dang it, Raider," he said, "I heard all them screams and I figured you must have gotten around to Rachel here. I just came by to see if you'd left any for me."

When they ignored him, he went out again, chortling to himself.

The Dutch farmers didn't smoke, drink, curse—they even believed music was profane. The long list of prohibitions in their life would have been hard for a townsman to observe—but not so much for a farmer who worked from sunup to sundown except the Sabbath Day, and who as a result didn't have much time or energy for sinful ways.

The men worked the fields, fenced with barbed wire, using plows drawn by a pair of mules or horses to turn the prairie sod. They harrowed the plowed earth and sowed seed. Their women worked. Their children worked. They worked and they prayed, hoping to bring in enough in summer and fall to last through winter.

Grasshoppers, drought, blight, spring frosts took their toll, but most of all the farmers feared the ranchers always to their west. These cattlemen had come to believe the rangeland was theirs, regardless of government land grants and settlement rights. These ranchers looked at plowing the prairie the way the Dutch farmers looked at sin.

When the party of cattlemen rode in, the farmers ran home for their guns—mostly needle guns and some old muzzle-loaders. Their children hid under beds and tables, and their wives helped with ammunition. Each family guarded its farmhouse, refusing to be drawn out by the depredations of the cattlemen as they tore up fences and trampled crops with their horses' hooves.

Ev Dowling and his men had brought two wagons with them, which they loaded well out of range of the nearest farmhouse.

Three oil lamps hung outside Toss Carter's barn. The men stood quietly by their horses while Toss spoke.

"We have three jugs of kerosene—more than enough. Two men to a jug. Just pour the stuff onto the walls of the ranch house. If you have to run, drop the jug on its side and the oil will pour out. But don't put a match to it. Soon as you're ready to light yours, somebody else will maybe still be pouring his and you'll burn him to a cinder. It ain't Carters we want to burn tonight, men. I'll be the one to put the match to it and no one else. You don't have to worry with me. I'll wait till you're all clear. Now, I ain't fooling. I seen a man die screaming 'cause some fool threw a match too soon. You ready, men? Let's ride out."

The pace was slow, since there was no moon out and they had to depend on starlight. But the men knew this country, most of them from boyhood, and they found their way and kept together in a bunch with a minimum of fuss and noise. When they saw the lighted windows of Gavin Dowling's ranch house in the distance, they stopped and watched for a long while.

Toss Carter finally broke the silence, his raspy voice starting out barely above a whisper but rising in volume and vehemence as he spoke. "That lying, murdering, thieving, whoring Yankee sheepfucker Gavin Dowling's gonna meet his deserved end tonight. This night is gonna mark the beginning of a new era for the people of Wolf Creek. Some of them is going to remember it with joy—that's us, the Carters. Some is going to look back on it in sorrow —that's them, the Dowlings. One day you men will be proud to boast you rode along tonight. This is the beginning of the end for the Dowlings on Wolf Creek. Let them go to California and dig for gold! There ain't room for them here. This is Carter country!"

The men raised a cheer.

Toss Carter went on, "It ain't only that Gavin coyote we're gonna roast tonight, men. That renegade Rebel, that traitor to the Old South, that informing, spying, back-shooting bounty hunter Raider's going to cook in the same juice as that horse-thieving, train-robbing Dowling." He inhaled loudly and deeply. "This air is going to smell purtier after them two is well roasted on all sides. I done talking. Less said from now on the better. The sound of voices carries at night. You know what to do, men. Leave the match striking to me."

They rode in closer, stopping once more several hundred yards from the house. They watched and listened for a spell before breaking up into three groups. Each group was in possession of a two-gallon crock of kerosene. The group of four men taking the back of the ranch house circled around.

Toss whispered instructions to the men in his group. "Ride in fast, men. Don't worry about noise then. Two men handle the kerosene jug. Rest of us cover the windows and doors with our six-guns to keep the rats inside." He waited and watched until he guessed the two other groups were in position and ready. Then he raised a high, clear, lonesome Rebel yell and they all charged.

As they galloped in, some of the horses saw the wire and slewed sideways to avoid it, the barbs tearing flesh of the riders' near leg. Other horses plowed right into the multiple strands of barbed wire stretched taut on posts in a wide circle around the ranch house. The wire strands snapped, and stakes were pulled from the ground and flattened by the strength of the galloping horses. The animals whinnied with fright, reared on their hind legs, and bucked, some unseating their riders. The three kerosene crocks fell and were spilled, all more than thirty yards from the ranch house.

The house lamps extinguished, Raider, Gavin, Rachel, and Everett fired from the windows at random out into the darkness. Pausing only to pick up the men who had been thrown from their horses, the Carters scattered into the night. Some of them rode for miles and still couldn't figure out what had happened to them in the blackness.

# CHAPTER NINE

Living arrangements had always been informal at
Pawnee Springs. When the Indians had the land—
and there were still some about, though most had
been recently removed to the Indian Territory—they
came and went, putting up and taking down their
temporary shelters. There was nothing in the place
except some small ponds of sweet water. Farther
west, they would have been precious as gold, but in
the Kansas prairies water was not that scarce. White
men came and went these days, erecting their temporary shelters. Some lived in tents, others slept beneath wagons, still other built sod houses with grass
growing on the roof, which slowly subsided back
into the earth after they were abandoned.

There was no reason for any man to be in Pawnee
Springs in particular. It was not what the place was
that drew men there (there were no women). It was
what the place was not. It was not a town with a
marshal. It was not a place where the county sheriff
or his deputies liked to go. It was not known to east-

ern busybodies and do-gooders. It was not near any-place else. And it was not a great loss if it had disap-peared by the time you got there.

"I thought I might find you here," Arthur Dowling said to his brother Martin. "It's getting near impossi-ble to rob a train with those Pinkertons and railroad guards all over the place. You been here long?"

"'Bout a week," Martin said. "I lost four men and took a scalp wound over in Dickinson County. We were beaten back. You'd need twelve men and a cou-ple of thousand rounds of ammunition to rob a train these days."

"It won't last," Arthur predicted.

"I ain't so sure," Martin insisted. "When the railroad companies see that this heavy guarding is stopping robberies—and it is—they'll make it stan-dard everyplace."

Arthur laughed. "There ain't nothing to worry about. There's always something to be took by the man who's willing to reach out and grab it. You and me are that kind of man. We'll always be in clover. Gavin, too. You seen him or heard anything about him?"

"Naw. He's all right. If they had laid hands on him, they'd be crowing about it. Might be he'll show up here soon too, the way things are. Lie low for a spell."

"It ain't like Gavin to lie low."

"Sure ain't," Martin agreed. "If that son of a bitch can find fire, he'll play with it."

Both men had quit going on raids with their elder brother some time before. He bullied them. He never wanted to hear what they had to say. He used them. It was just like being kids at home for them. They came to physical blows many a time but stopped short of shooting. By mutual agreement, Martin and Arthur split off on their own, realizing that Gavin was agreeing only because he expected them to come crawling back to him in a few months. That never happened. What did happen was that Arthur and Martin, no longer united against Gavin, fought with each other. They decided to go solo. Now when they ran into one another, they were genuinely pleased to see each other. It had been some time since all three had met together, and they were in the mood for a family reunion.

Pawnee Springs was a good place for that. Officially it was as dry as any town in Kansas, which meant you could buy a bottle of rotgut just about anyplace. The two brothers bought a bottle between them every day, raced horses for small bets while it was still cool in the morning, dozed, reminisced, argued, and wandered aimlessly around the small settlement on foot. A lot of men would have been bored, but for Arthur and Martin it was rest and relaxation from long, dangerous, hard-living months of robbing and riding and blowing their ill-gotten gains. For once, they needn't keep looking back over their shoulder all the time.

At the end of a week, Martin began to get restless. "I reckon Gavin ain't going to show. He could be up at Latrobe or maybe he's at home. Maybe he'll show here, but not for another month."

"I wouldn't mind riding up to Latrobe. More to do there than in this prairie dog city."

"I'm short of funds," Martin said.

"Hell, you're better off than me. I'm close to

broke. Want to do a job together on the way? Fix ourselves with a small stake?"

Arthur wasn't asking real questions, and his brother didn't bother answering them. Both knew what they had to do.

"If we take on a train, we'll need to get ourselves some men," Martin said after a while.

Arthur grimaced. "Let me think about it."

The two brothers rode north for two days before hitting the railroad. The railroad company had sold its land grants to farmers, and more farms had settled government-owned lands, so that the grass was plowed continuously almost a mile wide on either side of the tracks, with farmhouses here and there. The Dowlings stayed clear on the still remaining prairie, avoiding these farmers like they would lepers.

"They ain't even worth robbing," Arthur said disgustedly. "All they own is some chipped plates and brass lamps."

They saw a town up ahead, one of those new towns built by the railroad and eastern speculators to lure more settlers in. Some of them were already ghost towns, being slowly picked apart for the lumber. This one looked healthy enough, with busy stores lining the main street and a solid, prosperous bank.

"Ain't no way we could rob it," Arthur judged, as they rode slowly past the bank. "Right now, I'm willing to bet there's someone ready to poke a rifle through his window and cover us."

Martin's eyes slid along the house fronts. "There's

probably ten men doing it. Look at this place. There ain't even a goddamn saloon."

"We ain't got no money anyhow."

"I'm tired eating jackrabbits and prairie chickens and drinking water," Martin grumbled. "Man, we're living like coyotes. Next night the moon comes up, we'll be howling at it. Let's get off our horses here and see what we can do for ourselves. There's no knowing what we may find."

Arthur wasn't so hopeful, but he was in no hurry to rush back to the empty prairie. The two men were hardly off their horses when the town marshal, backed by two deputies with scatterguns, came by for a word.

"Where are you boys headed?"

"Just passing through, Marshal," Arthur said. "We thought we might stop and stretch our legs."

"Don't take too long doing it," the marshal told them. "There ain't nothing in this town for the likes of you, and there's plenty of us here who would like nothing better than a chance to run you out."

"This ain't a very friendly place," Martin observed.

"No, it ain't," the marshal agreed. "If I was you, I'd keep that in mind every minute more you delay here."

The marshal and his two deputies withdrew a ways up the street so the two men could make a graceful exit.

"I'd like to kick their butts," Martin said of the townsfolk in general as he swung into his saddle.

Arthur said nothing, mounted his horse, and rode slowly alongside his brother, showing they were not to be hurried but, all the same, leaving no doubt in anyone's mind that they were on their way out of town. Neither man felt any injustice in the marshal's harsh judgment of their character—in fact, they agreed with him. The lawman had made a point of not making this a personal confrontation, where they might feel obliged to fight for honor's sake. This was all right with them. They had nothing to prove and a lot to hide. They would be on their way.

As they neared the edge of town, a young man joined them, clearly a local farmer's son. They were friendlier to him than they normally would have been, wanting him close to them for protection in case anyone in town tried sniping at them, and also because this farmer might drop something worth knowing.

The young man was apologetic, embarrassed by the cold treatment of these strangers by his elders. He was attracted also by the way they looked—lean, mean, dangerous—very different from the hearty, open, honest, hardworking farming people in these parts, who were the best people in the world but perhaps not the most interesting to a young man curious about the world at large.

"Did the marshal say to keep moving?"

"Something like that," Arthur said. "People here ain't exactly the welcoming sort."

"They ain't usually so unfriendly," the farmer said, anxious to defend his folks' good name. "It's just that right now the railroad company has been warning us to expect drifters coming up this way. Seems the railroad guards have these train robbers on the run, and there's no telling where they'll show up next."

Arthur looked shocked. "Surely the marshal didn't take us for train robbers?"

"Oh, no, I reckon not," the young man said hurriedly. "That's not what I meant at all. It's just that he can't be sure, and he's a careful man. You see, tomorrow that gold shipment comes in by train to the bank, so the marshal is just a bit extra suspicious of anyone who happens by with no clear cause."

"I would be too if I were in his boots," Arthur said.

"The man has a job to do," Martin said righteously.

They asked no more questions and parted company with the farmer outside town. They rode through the farmlands until they emerged onto the grasslands. Having shot and cooked two jackrabbits over an open fire, they ate and passed what remained of the day resting in a small shady hollow. After dark, they headed back toward town on foot, leaving their horses on long tethers in the hollow. A new moon lit their way, but it was a long trek, skirting the edge of the farmlands. On a few occasions they walked right into unseen strands of barbed wire and swore softly but in great detail at the farming sons of bitches who had put it there.

It was well before midnight when they reached town, but it was dead as a doornail, not a light showing, not even a dog barking. They walked quietly on a side street that paralleled the main street and which would bring them to the back of the bank. Martin opened the catch of a side window with his knife blade; the two men climbed inside and slid the window down after them. They opened some desk and counter drawers but found no money. Moonlight

streaming through one window illuminated the steel
face of a massive safe.

"We'd need half a ton of dynamite," Martin esti-
mated.

"You'd blow part of this town away and that safe
would still be standing there," Arthur said.

They lay on a carpeted area and slept until first
light. The two Dowlings kept out of sight while some
workers waited outside for the boss to arrive and un-
lock the doors. He came, and they and he found
themselves looking at two unwavering six-gun barrels. They did as they were told, leaving the doors
open and moving behind the counters as if all was
normal.

"We're going to give you a good deal," Arthur
told them. "None of you gets robbed. None of you
gets hurt. You the manager?"

"I own the bank," the boss said.

"Good. You're going to like what I have to say,"
Arthur said. "We ain't gonna steal from your vault.
We won't touch your customers' money. All we want
is that shipment of gold. It ain't yours till it's safely
delivered. Ain't that the way it works?"

"Not until I've signed for it," the banker said.

"So if we steal it before you sign for it, then it's
not your loss? We ain't robbing you?"

"Technically, that would be correct," the banker
allowed.

"Bullshit technically," Arthur yelled at him. "Are
we robbing you? Yes or no?"

"No. It would not be my loss."

Arthur smiled a slow cruel smile. "So you see, we
ain't here to rob you of so much as a nickel. Us two
will just hunker down here out of sight but where we

can see all of you, and you lot do business as usual. Anything goes wrong we shoot all of you first thing. So make sure nothing goes wrong. You tip off any of your customers that something's wrong, you're all dead men, no matter what happens to us. You'll be the first to die. Is that food you got there?"

"It's my lunch," the bank worker said.

The Dowlings went after it like two hungry bears.

The two Pinkerton operatives lay back on the upholstered train seats and dozed. They had become bored with looking out the windows at the endless prairie rolling past, had tired of playing cards with each other, had read all the newspapers, had checked out all the passengers carefully without seeming to do so. They woke as the train began to lose speed, both suddenly alert for possible trouble. One pulled out his watch, looked at the time, and consulted a list.

"We're running right on time. We make a delivery here. Gold coins to the bank." He put the watch back in his vest pocket with a satisfied look. "This sure beats looking for shoplifters in a department store. My feet used to kill me at the end of every day."

The other Pinkerton laughed. "You had a fancy job. I was down on the lakeshore docks, guarding warehouses at night. The wind froze my ass in winter, and the skeeters ate me alive in summer. You think they'll keep us on the trains permanent?"

"So long as the railroad companies pay our fees, sure they will. Soon as they quit, Pinkerton will haul us away and send us to any man willing to pay. That Scotch bastard would put us at the bottom of a coal mine in order to collect fees."

"He ain't so bad. Mr. Pinkerton is a hard man, but

leastways he's honest—and that's more than you can say for most fellas hiring out detectives."

"That's for sure. Well, I have no complaints about this job. Except maybe it's hard to stay awake a lot of the time."

The train was now braking, and they went back to the car behind. A railroad guard was pulling a canvas bag by its neck across the floor to the side door. The conductor opened this door from the outside after the train stopped, and the two Pinkertons jumped down and looked around. They nodded up to the guard, who dragged the heavy canvas bag to the car edge and pushed it out onto the ground, where its impact made the coins chatter.

The conductor pointed out the bank, about fifty yards away. The guard jumped down and hoisted the sack onto his back. Bent almost double beneath its weight, he staggered along the dirt street, followed by the two Pinkertons, watchful, right hand in pocket.

In a farming town like this, they knew they didn't have much cause for concern. They didn't want to cause a spectacle either by walking along with their guns drawn. They knew that a fast, inconspicuous delivery was best—though a man staggering toward a bank with a heavy sack is never really inconspicuous.

One Pinkerton held the bank door open for him, and both followed him inside. There were no customers in the place. The train guard turned about and backed up to the counter, releasing his burden when he felt its solid wood behind him. Again, they heard the chatter of coins.

The guard turned around, took a sheet of paper

from his pocket, held up for inspection the unbroken seal on the wire constricting the neck of the canvas bag and said, "Sign here, please."

Martin Dowling popped up from behind the counter and leveled his six-gun in the middle distance between the three. Before they got used to the sight of Martin, Arthur Dowling emerged at the other end of the counter.

Arthur said, "Get out that door, jump on that train, and move out of here."

The Pinkerton nearest Martin fired, the bullet tearing through his tweed pocket and missing Martin's face by a hand span. Martin did not miss. His bullet in return struck the Pinkerton square in the chest, lifting the young man off his feet and throwing his body on the floor like something cast away.

Arthur did not wait. He squeezed home the trigger and caught the second man with his hand in his pocket high above the heart. He snapped back the hammer and put a second slug into him without really thinking about it. The gun was cocked and ready for a third shot before the Pinkerton's body collapsed on the floorboards.

Martin meanwhile was covering the uniformed train guard, who had a Smith & Wesson on his left hip and was keeping both his hands on the bank counter. The bank owner and his staff didn't make a move either.

"I'll get some horses," Arthur said.

Farmers who had heard the shots saw one of the men the marshal had run out of town the previous day come out of the bank and just take two horses, asking no one's leave, from the hitching rail outside the feed store. None of them felt up to challenging this hombre, but they did all start hooting and hollering to raise the alarm.

Several more farmers had come outside to see what could be going on when the second no-good drifter came running out the bank door with a heavy sack. It showed how strong he was—the train guard had been staggering beneath its weight, and this desperado was holding the sack in his left hand and running. They mounted the stolen horses and galloped out of town. The postmaster had a rifle, and he sent three shots after them, but he wasn't wearing his spectacles and put all three bullets in the dirt about twenty yards in front of them.

The marshal came running, and he organized the men into a posse. In less than twenty minutes, two dozen riders were galloping in pursuit. Many of their horses would have been more at home between the shafts of a wagon or pulling a plow than saddled as a riding horse; the farmers needed full-chested, heavy-hooved draft animals, not lithe, fast cow ponies. The big horses kicked up a storm of dust and made the ground tremble beneath them as the posse rode out, but half a mile farther on many of the animals were already wheezing from the pace and working up a lather of sweat.

The horses Arthur Dowling had stolen were no better, but both men beat them with their hats, yelled, and viciously spurred them. Unaccustomed to spurs, the horses ran in a wild, fear-stricken fury in the direction their heads were pointed. Both animals were at the point of exhaustion when the two men reached the hollow in which they had left their broncos.

They changed horses and headed north, losing no time. They knew they would be followed, and there were still many hours of daylight left. Many things could go wrong.

Passing close to a farmhouse, Arthur saw a woman watching them from the open door. Thinking they might not have seen her, she withdrew, leaving the door ajar. Inside Arthur saw the most beautiful sight his eyes had witnessed in days—a smoked ham hanging from a rafter. He unsheathed his bowie, jabbed the point through the canvas bag that Martin was carrying, and used two fingers to pick out a ten-dollar gold coin. He threw it in the open door and called to her to bring out the ham. She lost her shyness in a hurry. Arthur looped the string of the ham over his saddle horn and used the bowie to cut a thick sliver, which he passed to his brother. Munching on the salty, smoked meat, they headed steadily north out of the farmlands and onto the prairie.

They saw the posse behind them after about an hour, but they didn't speed up or slow down. One by one, riders dropped back from the posse. At sundown they were as far behind as ever, and their number was now reduced to ten men.

Arthur and Martin rode all night. At first light they could see no living man nor animal in any direction around them, only grass waving in the breeze. Most of the ham was gone.

# CHAPTER TEN

Everett wolfed down his breakfast and left at the crack of dawn to look after the cattle. Gavin didn't seem to get himself much involved with ranch work while he was home—he had other things on his mind, such as putting together a bunch of Dowling guns that could be called on in an emergency.

"It takes some of them bastards an hour to ride a mile when they hear there's trouble," he told Raider over a leisurely breakfast. "I want them to keep a fast horse in their corral at all times, have a saddle ready and a rifle loaded, and be able to find their boots when they roll out of bed. If the Carters thought there'd be a bunch of Dowlings riding down on them in quick time anyplace they raised hell, it'd be enough to turn their minds around and make them civilized beings again—as near as them Carter varmints can come to being civilized anyway."

"I'm not sure you're going about this the right way, Gavin," Raider said.

"It may not be the right way, but it's the *only* way.

I been brought up alongside these Carter side-winders. You better be wearing boots when you step on them."

Raider didn't bother to argue. He just sipped at his black coffee and waited for Gavin to leave.

But Gavin was in no hurry. "We got to put the fear of God in them, Raider, and me and you are just the men to do it. When you're on your feet again, we'll strike against them—hard. That will quiet them down till my brothers get here. After Arthur and Martin come, our family will be safe again. Then I can leave with you."

Raider nodded sardonically. He was having trouble seeing Gavin voluntarily turning himself in, especially with two gun-toting brothers to back him up if he decided otherwise. However, the pain in Raider's left leg instructed him to hold his tongue for the time being.

"I'm depending on you," Gavin said, "to keep the Carters from burning down this house while I'm out. That would be their move if you wasn't here—wait for me to step away for an hour and leave me without a roof over my head. Ev takes care of the stock real well, I got to grant him that. He seems to have struck his own private truce with some Carter boys, but sure as sundown, they'll stab him in the back. But he don't want to listen to me. So long as he cares for the stock, I suppose I got nothing to say. Same with Rachel here. So long as she cooks and keeps this ranch house clean, we gotta put up with her opinions. It ain't always easy to be reasonable with people like them, Raider, but I work on it even though I get no thanks or credit for it."

Rachel refused to be drawn in. She went about her

chores in silence, ignoring the two men sitting at the kitchen table.

Raider said nothing either, playing with his coffee cup and gazing out the window.

Seeing he was getting nowhere, Gavin pushed back his chair and said, "I best be pushing off."

Rachel and Raider said nothing to each other until they heard the thud of Gavin's horse's hooves.

"Is he gone?" she asked.

Raider watched him through the window, riding out onto the grasslands. "Finally," he said.

"Why don't you just shoot him and have done with it?" she asked. "He'd have back-shot you long since if he didn't need you. Once Martin or Arthur shows, he'll kill you with a smile on his face."

"I'm a Pinkerton, Rachel. That means I draw the line at murder and outlawry. Dang, I'm tempted as much as any man, and I guess sometimes I ain't as strict about toeing that line as I should be. But I don't shoot a man except in self-defense or to protect someone he's in the act of harming. Right now, it seems Gavin is set on nursing me back to health."

"That'll change soon enough."

"And that's when you'll see a change in me," Raider told her.

"I can't wait to see Gavin go," she said, "although I'll sure miss you." She walked over and held his head between her breasts. Then she released him and handed him his cane. She pointed to her bedroom door.

Raider hobbled in that direction, saying with a mock groan, "Well, off to work."

When they were in the bedroom Rachel shut the door behind them and shot home the two heavy bolts which she liked to say were there to "keep critters out." She unpinned her red hair, which tumbled down round her shoulders, and watched him with her green eyes as he shucked off his clothes and then lay on his back naked on her bed. She waited until he was settled and had his wounded, bandaged left thigh comfortable before she unhooked the back of her dress.

She disrobed fully and walked slowly across the room to the bed, taking her time so Raider could admire her body. She lay on the bed beside him and snuggled up to him. He turned on his right side, so they were pelvis to pelvis, and darted his tongue inside her mouth. He felt excitement surge through his body, and he cupped her firm, rounded ass in his hands.

Pulling her tightly to him, he let her feel the pressure of his stiff cock straining to get inside her. They spent some time like this, embracing and kissing in lustful abandon.

Lying on their sides, face to face, they explored each other's bodies with slow fingers. He felt Rachel guide his cock into her juicy sexual opening. The muscles of her vent closed around the head of his big penis. She let him enter her only an inch at a time while she excited her clit against his member.

She cried out and her body shuddered in orgasm even before he had sunk the full length of his cock into her depths. She trembled against him, moaned with fierce pleasure, and dug her nails into his back.

Gavin Dowling returned to the ranch house after a few hours. He looked from Raider to Rachel with suspicion and said, "You two look real cozy. I ain't interrupting anything, am I?"

"Sure you are, Gavin," Rachel snapped right back at him. "You're interrupting us human beings. Why don't you go out and stand in the corral?"

Gavin laughed. He was in a good mood. Besides, he'd been careful lately in the way he treated Rachel, insulting her—as she did him—but not going too far. He and Raider had had that out between them. The Pinkerton told him to watch his mouth, and Gavin accused him of having an affair with Rachel, which his brother Martin wouldn't be too pleased to hear. Raider said he wouldn't stand by and hear *any* man talk to *any* woman the way Gavin talked to Rachel. Gavin backed down real smooth, but Raider could tell by the glitter in his eye that when the day of reckoning came between the two of them, Gavin would have some scores to settle.

"Your wound all right?" he asked Raider.

"Rachel cleaned it and changed the bandage. Ain't no sign of festering, apart from being red and swollen."

"I'm gonna have you riding out with me soon. Those men I been telling you about are shaping up not too bad. First thing, they have to learn to take care of themselves, then they can look after other people. Some of them have a way to go yet. Damn, they're so slow-moving. If most of the Carters weren't slow and stupid too, we'd have been done for long ago."

He puttered around for a while, uneasy to be indoors. Finally he demanded to know where Everett was. When they said they didn't know, Gavin said he'd go find him.

It was just something to do. Gavin liked to keep busy—not working hard or anything like that, only he liked to be on the way to or from something, not wandering aimlessly. He had to know why he was someplace, that was all. Now he was looking for Everett. He had something to do.

He decided to look over a bunch of steers that caught his eye. From the brands on those nearest him, he could tell they were his. It does a man good to look over his property from time to time—Gavin was enjoying himself. His interest was caught by his horse's behavior. The animal's ears were twitching, it snorted a few times and pulled against the reins to look to the right. Gavin could see nothing that way. Yet he had spent enough years on the run, living on his wits and quick reactions, to grow mighty curious when his horse acted strange. Some horses were like humans, they imagined things and were scared of their own shadow. Not this one. Gavin decided to take a look. It might be a dead steer hidden in the grass or a calf with a broken leg.

He came to the edge of a steep-sided draw, which he had forgotten was there. Looking down into the dry streambed, on the sandy bottom he saw a sight that froze the blood in his veins. Gavin had been a lot of places, seen a lot of things, but not even his nightmares had prepared him for what was now before his eyes—his own youngest brother in the arms of a Carter woman!

His own flesh and blood turned traitor! The monstrosity of it rooted Gavin to the spot, leaving him almost breathless. He tried to shout and curse, but only a strangled croak came from his mouth. He drew his Peacemaker. The weight and steel of the gun steadied him down.

The girl spotted him and screamed. He threw a shot at her open mouth and missed. Then his damn-fool brother jumped in front of the bitch, doing the hero by protecting her. What was wrong with Ev? Why had he turned out like this? Gavin leveled the gun on him. It would be like putting down a sick horse. . . .

The girl dragged them both to the ground and Gavin's bullet passed over them. Then they were on their feet once more, zigzagging, and he missed Ev with his third shot. They got around a bend in the draw and a small branch cut off his horse's way. Figuring it would be quicker than riding around the branch, he dismounted and ran after them along the bottom of the draw. They came into sight again once he rounded the bend. Their horses were tethered a little ways on, and the two of them were running for them. Damn, he should have brought his rifle; they would have been easy pickings. Gavin stopped to steady his Peacemaker for a shot at Ev. He missed again.

He fired twice more at Ev as they mounted their horses. After he saw he'd missed, he ran back to his own horse to give chase. By the time he was in the saddle, Gavin saw they had split—Ev heading back to the ranch, expecting to draw Gavin after him, and the girl heading for Wolf Creek and Carter territory. After she crossed the creek, she would be safe. He reckoned he knew a way to cut her off. He spurred his horse into a full canter, taking a way in which the rolling grassland concealed him from both his brother and the Carter girl.

He had plenty of time to face down Ev on this back at the ranch house, and if Ev had lit out by the time he got back there, good riddance to him. It would save shooting the bastard. No man liked to have to shoot his brother, no matter what kind of low traitor he was.

He had a chance to catch the girl. Emma, her name was. The cunt had tricked his weak-minded brother with her seductions. Well, if he laid hands on her, he'd show her a few tricks too. He'd make the little bitch squeal like a stuck rabbit.

Emma Carter rode hard for Wolf Creek. She saw no one behind her, which came as a relief because her mare was old and slower than the three- or four-year-old bronco Gavin was riding. Ev had tried to give her his rifle when they parted ways, but she had refused it, not being much of a hand with a gun and believing he would be needing it more than she. But she kept pushing her mare, figuring she wasn't free of danger until she had forded the creek.

She was more worried about Ev's safety than her own. What would become of him? And even if they both escaped physical harm from Gavin, wouldn't he put a stop to their seeing each other in future? She dreaded this prospect as much as she feared Gavin's bullets. For her, it would be a slow death in place of a fast one from a gunshot.

Her horse began to tire, and she urged the animal on by calling out her name—Amanda—and patting her neck, which had the same or better effect than the sharp rowels of the spurs men wore, and some women too, though not Emma. She wasn't far from the creek when she saw Gavin outflank her from behind a rise in the ground. Her mare had no chance, and Emma reined her in, determined to face Gavin Dowling, and perhaps her own death, with dignity. In the back of her mind, she found it hard to believe that even Gavin Dowling would gun down a lone, defenseless woman if given time to think it over.

He brought his horse up to hers. "Get down," he said. "We have some talking to do."

Relieved to see that he was in a more reasonable frame of mind, she climbed down out of the saddle at the same time as he did. They let their horses rub noses and wander off a few paces together.

"So, you pleased with yourself, having dragged my little brother down in the Carter gutter?"

"You don't understand, Gavin."

"Ain't nothing to understand, cunt. 'Cept what's between your legs. You Carter women any different from others? Maybe I should take a look for myself to see what you got there."

He grabbed her by one arm and threw her on her back in the grass.

"Don't do this, Gavin," she pleaded. "You'll regret it."

"I never done a thing I regretted yet." He grinned. "I suppose it's time I started." He stood over her, looking down, still grinning, unbuttoning his fly. "You going to take your stuff off? That way it don't get tore."

"Amanda," she called.

"What?"

"Amanda!"

Her old mare dragged herself away from Gavin's colt in answer to her mistress's call. She lumbered straight for Gavin, who had to move fast to avoid being trampled. The mare was past her prime, but she was still a powerful animal, many times stronger and heavier than the most powerful man. The mare turned around and came at Gavin again. This time he quick-drew his Colt Peacemaker, thumbed back the hammer, leveled the barrel on the mare's neck, and squeezed the trigger. The hammer fell on a spent cartridge.

Gavin cursed, remembering now that he hadn't reloaded after emptying his gun on his fool brother. He had no time to reload his pistol now, not with this homicidal mare under the control of this Carter witch. He'd put the horse down painlessly and burn her at the stake, if he had his way in Webster County. But there was no time to think about such things now as the mare chased him away. His rifle was in his saddle sheath, but his horse was just standing there, not moving, watching all that was happening.

When he had been chased maybe fifty yards away, Emma called the horse to her, swung herself into the saddle faster than he had ever seen a woman do it before, and headed for the creek.

Gavin was so disgusted he didn't even try to catch her by running for his horse. He walked slowly toward his mount, kicking the long grass with his boots, pushing new loads into the chambers of his Colt. When he finally mounted his horse, he raked its sides with his sharp spurs until blood ran down its hide.

When Gavin walked in the door of the ranch house, he found Raider waiting for him in the kitchen. There was no mistaking the Pinkerton's intentions. Although he was crippled by his leg wound, he had taken a gunfighter's stance. He and Gavin didn't need words. Raider was telling him that if he had come back to do what Raider thought he had in mind, he first of all had about two hundred pounds of mean Pinkerton to blow away.

Gavin unbuckled his gunbelt and tossed it on the kitchen table. He watched Raider relax and laughed.

"That little bastard has been whining to you, ain't he?" Gavin asked. "Telling you about poking that Carter girl? Well, I hope his dick rots off."

Gavin poured himself a cup of coffee at the stove, then flopped in a hard-back chair. Raider limped back to his seat. Rachel opened her bedroom door a few inches and peered out.

"You ain't aiming to kill Ev no more?" she called out.

"Naw," Gavin said. "You can let him come out from behind your apron. Hell, I'm kind of surprised he even likes any kind of girl. I been wondering about him."

# CHAPTER ELEVEN

"You think he wants a truce?" one of Toss Carter's men asked.

Toss spat out of his toothless mouth and scratched the white stubble on his chin as he rode at the head of a dozen men to the schoolhouse in Bladen.

"Can't see no other reason for him wanting to talk with me," he answered. "He could have talked with any one of you if it was something easy to fix up."

The men saw the truth of that. For the present, the feud had come down to a struggle between these two men, Toss Carter and Gavin Dowling.

"You going to give him a truce, Toss?" one man asked.

"Sure. Until it's in our favor to fire the next shot." The men all laughed.

Toss continued, "That polecat is playing for time, waiting for the rest of his litter to show up. I'll give him any truce he wants, so long as his conditions is reasonable. We won't touch none of them Dowlings, abiding by our word. But the first man who can draw a bead on Gavin or on that renegade Southerner he's giving shelter to, he shoots him. That clear?"

They saw a bunch of Dowlings outside the schoolhouse, which was a kind of symbol of neutral territory for both sides. The Carters drew within two hundred yards of them and reined in when Toss held up his hand. Gavin rode slowly out to a point half-way between the two groups and pulled up his horse.

"This is real Indian style," Toss muttered and went forward to meet the challenge. He called back over his shoulder, loud enough for Gavin to hear, "If he plugs me, boys, don't let him ride away."

Both men were armed and came no closer than ten feet of one another.

Gavin said in a low voice, "I needed to talk with you so no one can hear. That's why I put word out on a truce. There won't be no truce ever between you and me, but there's something else you should know which matters to us both."

"Keep talking. I'm listening." Toss was surprised and curious to find he was not being swamped with some bullshit about peace between the two clans. He knew that would never come while he and Gavin were aboveground.

Gavin told him about catching Everett and Emma. He was pleased to see the shock on Toss's face and the slow spread of red over his cheeks and neck as his rage built.

"I don't know what you intend doing with your Carter girl," Gavin went on, without waiting for him to speak. "Maybe it's different for you if a woman's a traitor, though it ain't with me. I ain't got that problem to solve, 'cause it's my own brother who's our traitor."

"What you gonna do with him?" Toss asked after a pause.

"That's why I'm here."

"You ain't killed him yet?"

"No, though I tried hard enough when I found them," Gavin said. "Your Emma will testify to that. When I got back, that damn Pinkerton came down hard on me. I daren't touch the little rat. Rachel put the word out, and now none of my kinfolk will go near Ev either. They know that Pinkerton would cut them into coyote food."

Toss managed a toothless smile. "Seems like you have real problems with that Pinkerton man. We'd be doing you too much of a favor in killing him."

"Raider killed your nephew Hugh. I know you'll come after him for that, even if it does help me. Your urge for vengeance was always stronger than your good sense."

"My, my," Toss said, "we have a philosopher here. But I don't deny it, boy. So talk on."

"I ain't here to get you to kill that Pinkerton. You'll do it in your own good time, if we don't do it afore you. What I'm here to tell you is, first thing tomorrow morning, I'll send Ev in here to town. I'll wait till the last minute before telling him, so he won't have no one to go with him."

Toss thought this over in silence for a full minute. He finally said, "For you, you get rid of a no-good brother. For me, it's one less Dowling to put up with, though he ain't the worst of you by a long shot."

"Don't forget, Toss. He messed with a Carter girl."

Toss Carter's face darkened. "I ain't forgetting."

He swung his horse's head around and rode back to his men.

Next morning Ev was surprised by Gavin's order to head into Bladen right away and find someone who wanted to buy fifty horses. It was true their remuda had grown way too large for their needs, but this wasn't the best way to trim it down and Gavin knew it, unless he was losing touch with ranching from being away too much.

"We'd do better in price placing a dozen head here, another dozen someplace else," Ev said.

"Fifty," Gavin said. "And I want at least forty dollars a head for them, no paper money."

"Our own kinfolk along Wolf Creek will give us a better price than I can get for a big bunch in Bladen," Ev argued.

"So maybe we'll sell them some. First, see what you can do in Bladen."

They had given Ev the responsibility of running the ranch, and he didn't allow any of his three brothers to bully him in that one area. However, he was so pleased that Gavin was on speaking terms with him again that this one time he was willing to follow ranching instructions that he knew to be wrong. Maybe he could bring Gavin around to his way of thinking about Emma. If only Gavin got to know her, he might like and approve of her. Deep down, Ev knew this would never happen, since Gavin didn't treat women in a decent way. This morning, however, he was hoping, and, to be agreeable, he said he would go.

Ev tried to rustle up some company, but no one was around. He was about to go back in the ranch house to ask Rachel if there was anything she needed from town, but Gavin started hassling him for not being gone yet, so Ev saddled up and rode out with no more delay.

Ev was nearly halfway to Bladen, on the stretch that was close to Wolf Creek, when he saw a rider approaching him. Ev pulled his Winchester rifle from the saddle scabbard and levered a shell into the chamber. The rider nearing him did not take similar precautions, although he must have noticed what Ev was doing. Then Ev recognized him. His name was Phil Burke, and he had been to school with Emma and him. In fact, Ev was always a bit jealous of Phil, because he knew Emma and he were close friends, living close by one another and not having the stupid feud to keep them apart, like Emma and he did. Phil's mother had been a Carter, and he was brought up by them, his parents having died of a fever when he was a small child.

"Go back," Phil shouted to him. "They're laying in wait up ahead for you. Emma sent me."

"Is she all right?" were the first words that came to Ev's mind and lips.

"She got slapped around some by Toss last evening and her face is swole. She's sure he'll kill her, but he wants to get you first."

"Why did Emma tell him?"

"She didn't," Phil said. "Your own brother told Toss."

Ev almost choked with grief and shock. "Gavin said he met with Toss to try to talk peace with him and failed. All he was doing was telling him about Emma and me. He knew Toss would kill us both, do the job for him. Damn him to hell. I say that even if he is my brother. Damn him."

"You best be getting back," Phil suggested in a sympathetic voice.

"Bring Emma here tonight," Ev said on an impulse. "I'll meet you in this place an hour after dark. Have her bring her things, I'll have a second horse to carry them. We're gonna light out."

"Best thing," Phil said and headed away.

Ev went back the way he had come, worrying about the way Phil had immediately agreed to Emma's fast departure. Things had to be very serious for Phil to agree so readily to let his close friend Emma go. He was aroused from his reverie by shots. Thinking they were aimed at him, he lay low on his horse's neck and cantered the animal. Looking back, he saw two horsemen chasing Phil. All three were already on the Carter side of the creek. There was nothing he could do to help Phil—they were too far away already and on enemy turf.

These weren't Dowlings chasing Phil. Ev knew that right away. More likely, they were the ones who had been lying in wait for him. Phil Burke had spoiled their trap. Now they were out to get him.

Phil Burke rode like the devil. Noah Carter and Tommy Winthrop were chasing him, fellas his own age, who he had been to school with, who knew Emma and Ev. Now they would kill him if they could catch him. They might just as easily have chased Ev Dowling as him; after all, Ev was the one they had been waiting to kill on Toss's orders. But Phil knew why they had picked on him. He was an informer. It didn't matter how good his reason was to inform. All that mattered was that he had helped the enemy. And there was only one thing worse than an enemy, and that was someone who betrayed his own. So they came after him instead of going after Ev.

He whipped his horse with a length of rawhide and dug his heels into its ribs, but fast as he was going, the others were gaining on him.

Phil understood why they would want to kill him. He himself was a bit bewildered at how his loyalty to Emma and past friendship with Ev could so easily make a traitor of him. What could he have done? Say no to Emma and let Ev be murdered? No man in his right mind would have asked him to do that. But Toss Carter was not in his right mind, and the Carters who did stop and think were dead or wise enough to stay home and keep their doors and mouths closed.

He lashed his horse and peered back. Noah and Tommy were getting closer. Phil began to believe he had made a mistake, after being spotted, of continuing into Carter territory. This wasn't going to be home turf for him any longer. He wouldn't be welcome on Dowling land either. There was nothing now for him to do but leave along with Emma and Ev an hour after dark tonight. A bullet whirred past his left shoulder, a quarter second before he heard the shot.

Still riding hard, ever more fearful of the riders gaining on him, Phil never knew what hit him. It was a .45 lump of lead from Tommy's old Navy Colt, which clean severed his spine below the shoulder blades. His body loosely rolled down the side of his cantering horse.

"Nice shot," Noah said enviously, reining in and giving Tommy the credit.

Tommy looked down the smoking barrel of the Navy Colt at the head of his former classmate. He pulled the trigger and blew apart Phil's skull.

"Traitor," Tommy said.

"Scum," Noah agreed.

Ev Dowling walked in the ranch house door with his rifle leveled and ready to fire. If Gavin had been standing there he might have fired. He wasn't sure. But he might have. The kitchen was empty.

Ev noticed that Rachel's bedroom door was shut, which meant she was inside. He banged on it.

"What is it?" Rachel called.

Ev was puzzled. Her voice sounded funny. "I'm looking for Raider," he said.

"What makes you think he's in here?" she asked querulously.

A moment ago, Ev hadn't even suspected. Now he was sure. He knew Rachel, and Rachel's voice sounded like that for one good reason he could think of. He said, "I know he's with you, Rachel. Sorry to intrude, but I think Emma's in bad trouble and I need his help."

That brought both of them out after a few minutes, Raider looking the same as always, but Rachel flushed and her hair not as carefully pinned up on her head as usual.

"I dunno what's coming over young people in these parts," Toss Carter complained on hearing what happened from Tommy Winthrop and Noah Carter. "Phil and Emma both turncoats on our side, Ev on his. I believe it's the example of that renegade Southern Pinkerton over there in the Yankee camp. He's infected them. He's the rotten apple in the barrel. But you two young fellas done right. Us Carters can depend on you two to see things straight and do what needs to be done."

"What you going to do about Emma?" Tommy asked.

"Shoot the little bitch," Toss snarled.

"You are? " Tommy asked, surprised.

"No, *you* are," Toss told him. "I'm telling you what to do."

"I ain't gonna shoot no girl," Tommy said.

"Me neither," Noah added.

Tommy picked up again. "Killing a woman ain't a thing a real man does, even when she's a traitor."

"Besides, it ain't like a man being disloyal," Noah explained. "Women think different. They don't have sense enough to see things the way we do. You have to make allowances for them."

"You boys are fools," Toss growled, "and I been around long enough to know it's a waste of time arguing with fools, especially on the subject of women. The less a man knows about them, the more he has to say. But I can respect your feelings on this subject."

Toss was more than a little annoyed at the two young men for standing up to him. They never would have done so only a short while previously, but now that they had drawn blood they thought they were men. Toss decided he would bide his time with them. He'd give them their head for a while and then rein them in hard when they needed it.

"Talk about respecting feelings and so forth," Toss went on, "I reckon it's only you and me who know what really happened. Ev Dowling too, of course, but he don't matter. You talk with anyone before me?"

"No, we come right here," Noah said.

"Anyone else might have seen you out there?" Toss asked.

"Just Ev."

Toss nodded with satisfaction. "That son of a bitch Ev Dowling shot Phil Burke. You two boys seen him do it from far away. Ev run off when he saw you coming. You knew you couldn't catch him, so you came here to me. Get yourself a spare horse and fetch his body back to his place. I'll be there waiting for you. I'll have broken the news. His ma and pa are passed over, so it will be easy. There's only his sister, Wild Margie."

Tommy and Noah turned to leave.

Toss called after them, "Be much easier on you two not to have killed Phil Burke. There's too many who liked him. He was always with Emma. Folks will believe, now they've heard about Ev Dowling meeting her in secret, that he killed Phil in a jealous fit."

Tommy smiled. "That's right clever of you."

"We saw Ev do it," Noah said.

What looked like rolling grassland with no shade and no hiding places mostly was. Yet in some areas streambeds, hollows, hillocks, and long swells of land could provide cover for a whole bunch of horsemen. The Indians had used such places to mount surprise attacks. From a ways off, these places all looked like the rest of the grassland. Only up close was the deception plain.

Ev Dowling led Raider along these draws and

hollows and small ridges, mostly out of sight. They forded Wolf Creek and continued along more draws and gulleys. Their horses went at walking pace on the uneven ground. Even so, Raider's mount stumbled frequently on holes and misstepped on slopes, jolting him in the saddle and causing blinding pain to shoot up his wounded thigh into his lower body. The Pinkerton held a short length of rawhide crosswise in his teeth; each time the pain streaked like lightning through his system, he squeezed his eyes shut and bit down hard on the rawhide. The strip of rawhide was well chewed by the time they neared the spread where Emma Carter lived.

Raider was surprised at this unsuspected daring on the part of Ev Dowling. It seemed the young man, spurred on by love, thought nothing of riding by broad daylight into the middle of Carter territory, where his discovery would almost certainly result in death. He told Raider in a matter-of-fact way that when he and Emma didn't meet someplace out on the range he would make this trip to her place and she would sneak out to meet him in the hayloft of the barn. He'd had a few close calls but never been caught.

"Me and Emma was always friends at school," he told Raider. "When we finished there, it was a surprise to me that I missed her like hell. I thought it would pass. It didn't. I found myself riding nearer and nearer her spread, from the direction of the open range, hoping I would lay eyes on her. One day I felt plumb crazy enough to just ride to her place, finding my way along these draws. I spent hours hiding in the hayloft, waiting until she stepped by alone. When she heard me call to her and looked up and saw me in the loft, I saw by the look on her face that my risk had been worthwhile. I didn't have to explain nothing to her. She understood and didn't think it was crazy, either—though I myself was wondering."

Raider was impressed, and he wasn't an easy man to impress. He realized now that Ev was just as tough and resolved as his brother Gavin. At first Raider had gone along with Gavin that his kid brother was soft and hiding behind Rachel. Rachel had known all along about Emma. Emma had even visited the ranch house when none of Ev's brothers were around, which was most of the time. Ev's game had been to offer no resistance to his three brothers, knowing he only had to outwait them, that they would grow restless and leave again after a short time.

They tied the horses to a thicket in a draw. Taking their long guns, Ev led the way toward the house, which they couldn't see. Raider had to be helped down from the saddle and leaned heavily on his cane as he plodded along behind Ev, his teeth clamped tightly on the rawhide strip.

"I sure appreciate what you're doing for me," Ev said to him.

Raider grunted. He didn't like this kind of talk.

Ev looked at the badly limping Pinkerton critically. "I guess we don't have any plans for a quick getaway."

With the rawhide in his mouth, it was hard to tell if Raider smiled.

They made slow progress and came out into the open behind the house, which had no windows in its back wall. The barn was to the left of the ranch house, with only a small yard space between them. They walked into the barn without having to pass a house window, though anyone casually coming or going couldn't have missed seeing them. It might have been less risky for a quick-moving, slight young man like Ev. For a six-foot-two Pinkerton with a game leg, the chances of being seen were greatly increased. Inside the barn, Raider had to climb a ladder to the hayloft.

One part of the loft was stacked with hay, the rest used as storage for odds and ends, such as branding irons, coiled lariats, old saddles and harnesses. An opening for pitching hay down to the yard looked out onto the front of the house. Ev leaned their long guns against the wall, one on each side of this opening.

"I hope they ain't already done something to her," he said.

Raider said nothing.

"I guess we just wait," Ev said. "When she comes out, I'll call to her. She'll behave like she don't hear me, then in a few minutes she'll be up here."

Raider smiled and nodded. He hoped it was going to be that easy, but if he had believed it would be that easy, he would have let Ev go fetch the girl on his own. He agreed with Ev that Emma was in danger and that she had to be gotten out. In Ev's opinion, she would refuse to come, because of the old aunt she was looking after.

They were there for more than an hour without anyone showing or any sign of life in the house.

"Her aunt's a cripple and housebound," Ev said. "She does all right on her own for hours at a time, but she can't cook or move about so good. Emma reads to her a lot, or maybe Emma is in town or visiting with someone. She'll be back."

In a while, they heard a horse's hooves. A tall,

thin girl rode it. Ev tensed when he saw her.

"That's Wild Margie," he whispered to Raider. "She's Phil Burke's sister. And she ain't called wild for nothing. She's got more nerve than most fellas and don't mind talking her mind to anyone."

The tall, thin girl didn't look too wild to Raider. Tears were streaming down her cheeks. Still in her twenties, she wasn't pretty but not ugly either.

"Emma!" she hollered. "Emma! You come out here right now!"

A lace curtain in a front window was pulled open a little, then fell back in place.

"I know you're in there!" Wild Margie shouted, bringing her horse to a standstill directly beneath Raider and Ev's vantage point.

The ranch house door opened and a pretty young woman came out.

"That's Emma," Ev whispered to Raider and looked at him to see what the Pinkerton thought of her.

"She looks real nice," Raider said in an undertone to shut him up.

Ev looked pleased.

Wild Margie shouted, "Phil's dead. He's been shot."

"Oh, my God," Emma said and began weeping.

"It don't seem to come as a big surprise to you, Emma."

Between sobs, Emma said, "It's my fault. I asked him to warn Ev that Toss had some of our boys laying in wait to kill him this morning."

"It was Ev that killed him," Margie half screamed.

"No, it wasn't," Emma shouted. "Why would Ev shoot him? Phil was helping him."

"Liar! You lying Jezebel, you were two-timing Phil with Ev. Phil was in love with you."

"Maybe he was," Emma conceded, "but he knew all along about Ev and me. He was the only person who did. Oh, I'm so sorry, Margie. Poor Phil. It happened because he tried to help us." She began to walk toward Margie with her hands held out. "Please come down off that horse and come inside. I'll tell you everything."

This was not what Margie wanted to her. "You don't fool me, Jezebel!' she shouted and hauled a single-barrel scattergun from her saddle sheath. "You fool around with some no-good Dowling stud and he kills my brother in a jealous fit. I reckon blood has to be answered with blood. This time it's your blood, Jezebel." She raised the scattergun.

From above her, Raider was aiming with his .44 pistol at the stock of the girl's scattergun. He held off squeezing the trigger only because he saw Ev, from the corner of his eye, twirl a lariat. The braided rawhide lariat snaked out through the hayloft opening, and its noose dropped neatly over the mounted girl's head and shoulders. When Ev drew hard on the noose to tighten it, the rawhide pinioned Margie's elbows to her body, caused the scattergun to fall from her hands, and pulled her out of the saddle.

While she struggled to her feet and attempted to loosen the noose, Ev jumped to the ground from the hayloft opening. He threw a few turns of rope around Margie's body, pulled hard, and laid her in the dirt, squirming and helpless as a calf. However, no long-horn calf ever had a mouth to match Margie's. She cursed Ev up and down, this way and that—and even used some words Raider hadn't heard in quite a while.

It took Raider some minutes to get down from the loft by way of the ladder with their long guns. Margie shut up when she saw him.

Raider said, "Emma, get your things. It ain't safe here for you no more. As you can see, Margie was sent to kill you. Get your things."

"But who'll take care of my aunt?" Emma asked.

"Margie will," Raider told her.

The two women looked at each other for a moment, then Emma went in the house.

Raider spoke in a low voice to the trussed-up girl on the ground. "Margie, Ev didn't kill your brother. Tell her who did, Ev."

"Noah and Tommy."

Raider unwound the lariat from around her and helped her to her feet. He handed her the loaded scattergun. She put it in the saddle scabbard, accepted his help into the saddle, and rode away.

When Wild Margie arrived home, she left her horse at the door and walked in. Phil's body was still stretched on the kitchen table, where Tommy and Noah had laid him when they brought him. Some of the neighbor women were getting the body ready for burial, putting the head and face back together as best they could and picking off the crusts of dried blood from the skin. Their menfolk were at the other end of the kitchen, passing a jug among them. Toss, Noah, and Tommy broke off from the others and stood in a corner by themselves, waiting for her to come to them. She let them wait.

Wild Margie didn't have a high opinion of folks in these parts, and she let them know it. Rather than face up to what she was telling them, they preferred to think she was a mite crazy. Margie was proud to have an independent head on her shoulders and cared not a hoot what folks said so long as she could have her own thoughts on the matter. What the Pinkerton said had shook her up. He had stuck to a few bare facts, and she could take them or leave them. He hadn't tried to butter her up, like Toss had done. Maybe she had been a fool to believe Toss. She wasn't quite sure yet.

Surprised that she was able to look at the mangled head of her brother, whom she had loved dearly, she joined the women around the kitchen table. They held her hands and commiserated softly with her. On the table beside the body were two lumps of misshapen lead.

"You took these from the body?" she asked.

"One from his head, one from his back."

She picked up the bullets, sticky with blood. Having taken Winchester rifle bullets out of jackrabbits before cooking the meat, she knew well what they looked like. These bullets were heavier, like .45s. Ev never carried a .45 pistol, nor had he been wearing one an hour ago. He had a Winchester rifle. If Ev had killed Phil, these should have been the smaller-caliber Winchester bullets. She looked across the kitchen. Both Tommy and Noah had .45 revolvers in their gunbelts.

She left the table and went to the three men in the corner.

"How did it go?" Toss asked her in a low voice.

"Ev and the Pinkerton got there before me. They

tied me with a lariat and left with Emma."

"How long ago?" Toss asked urgently. "Can we catch them?"

She shook her head.

"I thought Raider was shot in the leg and couldn't walk," Noah said.

"He was walking with a cane," Margie said. "In his left hand."

They didn't have much to say after that, and she went outside to stable her horse. Seeing the scatter-gun still in the saddle scabbard, she drew it out to bring it in the house. As she walked in the door, Toss and the other two were talking together in the corner. When they saw her coming with the gun, the same look of guilty alarm crossed all three of their faces. Noah's hand closed on the handle of his gun. Margie passed them by and stood the scattergun in a corner.

It was their reaction to her at that moment that confirmed the truth in her mind about who had killed her brother.

Raider rode into Bladen with Emma and Ev. He arranged for Emma to stay with Lorna Carter and her mother, above the eating house. Word would spread fast where Emma was, but she would be safe enough so long as she stayed in town. Ev was all for just riding west and never looking back, but Emma wouldn't hear of it until she heard about how her aunt was being cared for. Ev got stubborn then and said he wasn't going to hide in town, he was going back to the ranch, regardless of Gavin or anybody else.

Raider's leg was paining him so bad after all the day's riding and walking, he said he didn't give a damn anymore what anybody did. He lay down on a spare bed over the eating house and said he wasn't going to move again until tomorrow, if then. In spite of everyone's advice, Ev left after dark for the ranch.

When things were quiet and the town was sleeping, Lorna paid Raider a visit. She lay beside him and let him hold her close.

"I been jealous," she confessed.

"Why?"

"You're out there with that red-haired Dowling woman," she said. "I know Rachel. Don't try to tell me she ain't friendly to you."

"She's a friendly person," Raider said noncommittally.

Lorna gave him a playful slap. "That's not what I mean, and you know it."

"Oh, you mean that kind of friendly," he said. "Well, maybe she would be if it weren't for my game leg. That kind of puts a stop to things."

"It might stop a Dowling girl," Lorna said, "but it ain't gonna stop a Carter girl like me."

Raider couldn't help feeling that maybe playing both sides of the feud like this wasn't the smartest thing he'd ever done in his life. But these feelings gradually went away as he lay on his good side and let his hands rove over the soft smooth skin of Lorna's body, and as he felt her hands glide over him and her gentle fingers enclose his cock.

# CHAPTER TWELVE

Ev arrived at the ranch house after midnight. The ride from Bladen in the dark had taken a long time. If he hadn't known the way so well, he'd never have found the house. A lamp burned in the kitchen window, which he assumed Rachel had left for him. He searched in the moonlight for the gap in the barbed wire fence around the house. He had driven three steers as payment to the farmer he had taken the wire from, which kind of dumbfounded the farmer. He came in the door with his Winchester ready, wondering if Gavin would try to kill him. Ev knew that his brother would have heard his horse and would have checked who was there. With the house door left unlocked, he knew Gavin would be awake and watching. Gavin was. He was sitting at the kitchen table, reading a newspaper he had gotten someplace. He surprised Ev by looking up with a big smile on his face.

"I hear you gunned down Phil Burke," Gavin said.

"No, I didn't."

"He's dead," Gavin said.

"I didn't kill him."

Gavin shrugged. "Don't make a difference. All them Carters believe you done it, and that's what counts. From now on, they'll be gunning for you same as for me. Me and you is in the one boat now. We'd better pull together."

Ev stood his rifle in a corner, noticed that Rachel's door was closed, and took his time about sitting down. "I was thinking I might ride out of here."

Gavin looked surprised and genuinely concerned. "Where would you go?"

"West."

"Why would you do that?"

Ev took his time answering. "I ain't scared of those Carter assholes, and I'm done being frightened of you, too. I been running this ranch for you since I was a kid, and I get nothing for it except suspicion from you that I'm stealing from you. I know enough to hire out as a top hand with some outfit or maybe even manage a spread for one of them big cattle companies and raise some stock on the side for myself. I know how it's done. I'm thinking it's about time I quit putting up with horseshit from you and them crazy Carters and put together a life of my own."

To Ev's surprise, Gavin pounded his fist on the table and said, "Damn me but them's words I like to hear. I was wondering when you was going to wake up and be a man. My baby brother has finally growed. Took a killing to do it."

"I didn't kill Phil Burke."

"Folks think you did. It's what folks think means everything, not what you do behind their backs."

"Gavin, me and you don't see eye to eye on things," Ev said.

"I don't expect you to. Now you're your own man, Ev. You want to know what's here for you in Wolf Creek. That's a fair question. This spread is yours. Any fool could have told you that. Me and Arthur and Martin ain't no good. If any one of us stayed here long enough, the law would hunt us down. I got Raider on my coattails this very moment. If us three don't get shot or hung, we'll end up in the Indian Territory or over the river in Mexico. Our time is running out, Ev. Like them farmers moving in on us cattlemen and fencing off the rangelands. Well, them lawmen is moving in on us badmen and putting us behind bars. Things are changing fast. Too fast. You're the one with the future, Ev. I'm the one with the past. You stick it out and everything'll end up yours."

Ev tried to control the emotion he felt for his brother. "That's strange talk, coming from a man that tried to have me killed only this morning. I know what you told Toss Carter and why you sent me to town."

"I reckon I was mad at you over that Carter girl."

"And now?"

"I ain't pleased, but I ain't mad."

Ev knew that was as much as he would get from his brother in the way of an explanation. He realized too that Gavin was telling him the truth. That was how he dealt with people—either they did what he wanted or they made him mad.

"Where's that lawman?" Gavin asked cagily. "He been helping you?"

Ev ignored the second question. "He's staying the night in Bladen to rest his leg."

Gavin was interested. "Has it got bad?"

"No, he's managing real good."

"Reckon I'm gonna have to watch out for him in the long run," Gavin said thoughtfully. "But I got this feeling you and me are going to need him real soon, unless Martin and Arthur show."

"He'll be back tomorrow."

"I'm going to sit up all night and watch this place," Gavin said. "You best get some shut-eye. You're going to need your rest. Looking over your shoulder all the time takes a lot out of a man."

Lorna was still beside Raider when he woke next morning. She was sleeping peacefully with her face on his shoulder, and he didn't want to wake her, except her mother might be wondering where she was if she woke early. Raider didn't mind tangling with murderous horse thieves, but he didn't know how to handle people's mothers. Normally mothers outright disapproved of him, which made things easy for him —all he had to do was avoid them at any cost. Lorna's mother actually seemed to like him, which worried Raider in case the woman had made the mistake of thinking he was a suitable marriage prospect for her daughter. When that crossed his mind, he hurriedly woke Lorna.

"My mother don't care," Lorna said sleepily. "Unless she's a fool, she's already guessed I'm with you. And she's no fool."

Raider stayed restless until Lorna tried a few things to distract his mind. She soon had his dick standing at attention. While he lay on his back, she straddled him. He held both her breasts in his hands while she lowered herself slowly onto his erect prong. She gasped as he pierced her. He could feel her soft flesh quivering as his shaft's full length sought out her core. Then she rode up and down his great stiff cock, like a rider on a pitching bronco.

After a feed of eggs, bacon, and sourdough biscuits, Raider walked down to the stables to get his horse. He was walking better today, with less pain than yesterday. He resolved to stay on his feet every day from now on, his days of being an invalid over. Raider more than half believed that making allowances for his wound would only make it worse. He tried to get to the stables without using the cane as a support, and almost made it. He staggered with pain and barely managed to stay upright the last twenty paces, propped with the cane. After resting for half an hour, he climbed into the saddle and rode slowly out of town for Wolf Creek.

He soon left the last of the outlying cabins behind, and it wasn't long before the town dropped out of sight behind him and he was alone in a sea of grass. Still nauseous from overstraining his leg at the stables, Raider passed the time by impatiently cursing his wound. After a while, this made him feel better.

He was almost back to his old self when he spotted two horsemen on his right. They were riding in the same direction as he was and slowly cutting in closer to him. Raider loosened his six-gun in its holster, knowing this was no casual encounter.

When they came closer, Raider saw two very young men, swaggering riders, who parted by about ten yards so he couldn't nail both of them with two quick shots, if he had a mind to. The Pinkerton was amused by their antics, seeing plainly the nervousness beneath their exaggerated self-confidence and knowing the uselessness of their maneuver for men who were not dead-eye sharpshooters. That they should try to intimidate him like this told Raider they were still only boys, lucky so far to have run into no professional gunfighters. It was always youths like these who died like dogs in the dirt or on sawdust floors, having believed in their own powers too much and in the experience of older men too little.

"You boys hoping to put a notch on your guns?" he asked them in a relaxed friendly way.

"We done that already," one said to him.

"So I heard," Raider answered. "Phil Burke was his name, wasn't it?" The look on their faces told him he had guessed their identities right. "Noah and Tommy, ain't that so? Well, I guess if you boys are ready to draw, I am too."

They looked at one another, then back at him. "You got us wrong, Mr. Raider," one said.

"Which one are you?"

"Tommy."

"Well, Tommy, I ain't got you wrong at all. You make one bad move, one quarter inch of a bad move, and I'll be happy to blast you. How does that sound to you?"

"We just wanted to ask you to come over to us," Tommy said. "You hail from the South, where we come from. Why ain't you on our side, instead of with them damn Yankees?"

"I ain't with the Dowlings, any more than I'm against you Carters. I come for Gavin Dowling.

When my leg's healed, we leave. Maybe you're forgetting it was your crowd who gave me this leg wound. I nailed some of your fellas, so that squares it with me. You Carters keep away till I'm gone and we won't have no more differences. But like I said, make one bad move—any of you—and I blast you."

"We don't see it your way, Mr. Raider," Tommy said.

Raider saw that what he had said had been wasted on them. They had come to take him on and were only trying to work up their nerve, maybe hoping to see some sign of weakness from him, which would be their signal to go for their guns. They were still wide apart, trying to swagger like they figured hardened gunslingers should.

"Then it's time you made your move, Tommy," the Pinkerton said in his easy, friendly voice. "Or are you going to draw first, Noah? Don't keep me waiting—or I might draw on you, and then you're both done."

They knew he wasn't joking. It was plain he thought he could shoot them both with no trouble. That friendly voice of his spooked them worse than what he said. What worried them both was maybe he could kill them.

"Ain't no use talking with him," Noah said to Tommy.

"Let's ride back," Tommy said.

As they rode away, Raider couldn't help grinning after them. He knew they hadn't left because they were smart, only because they were yellow. And he knew they would try to get back at him some way without facing him.

•      •   •   •

"You smell of that Carter bitch," Rachel hissed at Raider as soon as he came in the house.

"You mean Lorna?" he asked innocently.

"Yes."

"The sheets I slept on were perfumed, I guess," he said. "Nice smell. Like roses."

"When did you last smell a rose?"

He had to think about that. "I can't even remember the last time I seen one. But I remember them down in Arkansas when I was a kid. An old lady used to grow—"

"Did you sleep with Lorna?" Rachel was mad as hell.

"You're forgetting. I'm an invalid."

"That didn't stop you with me."

Raider smiled. "No Carter girl would be as clever as you to figure how we could manage it."

That quieted her, and he went outdoors before she got to questioning him again. Gavin and Ev came riding in together, something Raider hadn't seen before.

"I been telling Ev his days of riding the cattle alone are gone," Gavin said. "We run across some Carters and they steered clear of us."

"I ran into Noah and Tommy on the way from town," Raider said. "They were thinking about killing me but changed their minds."

Gavin laughed, understanding immediately what had taken place. Ev looked puzzled.

"Toss pushes them into doing stuff," Gavin said. "He talks them into believing they're mean hombres."

"The little sons of bitches are mean all right," Raider said, "but hombres they ain't."

The rest of the day passed quietly. That night, while Rachel was clearing the dishes from the table after supper, a bullet crashed through a windowpane next to her. At first, it looked like the bullet had knocked a plate from her hand, but afterward it turned out she had dropped the plate out of fright. The projectile buried itself in a log of the far wall.

Raider and Gavin doused the lights. Then the three men snuck outdoors with their long guns and waited.

"The bastards are maybe no more than a hundred yards from us," Gavin whispered.

"In another hour, the moon will be up," Ev said.

Raider lay on his belly staring into the darkness, listening.

For a while, nothing happened. Then they saw a spurt of flame about two hundred yards off to their right, and a bullet thudded into a log next to a window.

The Pinkerton was ready and waiting. He knocked off quick shots at where he had seen the muzzle flash and was rewarded with a howl of pain.

Raider rolled away fast to the right, so that when a hail of fire came from at least six rifles, he was no longer where they were aimed.

The man Raider had hit began to holler for help. He got taken out all right, but only after the three men outside the ranch house warmed their gun barrels well on the rescuers. When the half-moon rose, the Carters were gone.

"Think we got any more of them, Raider?" Gavin asked.

"We made at least a few of them piss in their pants," Raider said.

Raider stayed watch that night. There was no more trouble. They were finishing breakfast next morning when a bullet came through another window. When they rushed outside, they saw a lone horseman riding hell for leather a long distance away. Less than an hour later, they heard the smack of a bullet on the outside of the log wall. Again, a distant horseman.

"I guess I best start making window shutters," Gavin said. "I can use some boards from the barn wall."

"How about our stock?" Ev asked. "There's nothing to stop them shooting cows sporting our brand."

"Them Carters ain't that dumb," Gavin told him. "I'd leave them with a heap of dead beeves of their own. No, the ones they want bad is me and Raider. They won't try nothing with the stock while we're about. I best get moving on them shutters."

"Hold off awhile," Raider said. "You have a ladder in the barn, Ev?"

They put the ladder against the roof of the ranch house. Raider climbed painfully up it.

"Damn, I ain't had to do so much acrobatics in years," he growled, "and I have to do it on a bum leg."

He crawled onto the roof and up to its peak. He lay there on his belly, his carbine by his side.

"Raider, I ain't sure that roof was built to hold your weight," Gavin called up to him.

"Then you go inside. With any luck, I'll land on you."

After an hour in the sun, the Pinkerton felt like one of the crisp pieces of bacon for breakfast that morning. The sweat leaked through his shirt and jeans and trickled down the roof shingles. He kept the carbine in his body's shade, so the barrel would stay reasonably cool. When he did see a rider, he was coming from the side on which Raider lay. Without rising from his belly, he eased himself onto the far side of the roof, took off his hat, and peered over the top.

The rider looked like maybe he wasn't coming toward the ranch house after all. Then suddenly, apparently having decided all was clear, he galloped his horse right at the house and closed the distance fast.

Raider levered a shell into the carbine's firing chamber and bided his time. He knew how easy it was to jump to wrong conclusions and shoot an innocent man. First he wanted to be sure of this rider's intentions, and second he wanted him to come as close as he was willing without scaring him away.

The rider was no fool. He reined in his horse at long range and drew the rifle from his saddle scabbard. He didn't have to come closer, since a house is one hell of a lot easier to hit than a man on horseback. Raider heard the smash of glass as a bullet hit the window below him. He fired back, missing the rider by yards. He knew he had no chance of hitting him, so he went for the horse.

The roof gave him a longer shooting time than if he had been on the ground. His fifth shot in a row brought the horse down. He emptied the magazine as the man ran across the grass.

Raider didn't have to shout. Gavin came running from the house, tore off one top rail from the corral, leaped on a horse bareback, and spurred it to jump the two lower rails. He streaked across the grassland after the man on foot. The man had no chance. Gavin leveled him with two shots from his Peacemaker.

Raider saw Gavin dismount and appear to be helping the downed man, but after a couple of minutes he remounted his horse and returned. Raider climbed slowly down the ladder. When he came round to the front of the house, Gavin was nailing a blood-drenched scalp to the outside wall.

# CHAPTER THIRTEEN

All the funerals lately had been Carter funerals, along with the man Raider had shot in the dark outside the ranch house being laid up with a smashed left shoulder. The pendulum had swung. Now it was the Carters' turn to grow cautious and worry about being overrun. Toss's exhortations fell on deaf ears. It was all very well for him to go on about grinding the filthy Yankees into the dirt, but that was easier said than done with Gavin and the Pinkerton there. The last man to die had been a big blow. His horse had come home riderless, but they didn't find this body until two days later, where the buzzards were feeding and spiraling. They had torn his eyes and tongue out, but it wasn't the buzzards who had scalped him. The Dowlings in particular, and Yankees in general, dropped even slower in Carter estimation after this, but it was also true that some of the Carter men seemed to lose heart for the feud. Things got quiet.

Raider rode out every day to look at the stock and

to check on things in general. In spite of Gavin's warning, he mostly rode alone. Riders that shied away from him he assumed were Carters, and those that waved their hats to him Dowlings, but he couldn't be sure. Those riders he happened to talk with made it clear when they were Dowlings; when they left it unclear, he had to assume they were Carters, curious for a word with him for themselves —yet he could never be sure who was who. The man claiming to be a Dowling might be a Carter looking for a close shot. It would be fair to say that Raider didn't exactly grow sleepy on these rides.

The wound in his left thigh was mending well. No infection had set in, the swelling was less than a third of what it had been, and he could now ride for hours and feel only a dull, throbbing pain. He rode into Bladen one day to send a report to Chicago, knowing that if headquarters didn't hear from him soon they would send a search party. He gave them all the facts, including the one about his being shot in the left thigh. He insisted he didn't need backup. Guessing they would probably go against him on this, he intended to be clear of Wolf Creek and Bladen, with Gavin Dowling in tow, by the time any so-called help arrived. Raider liked to work alone; since this was the case, the Chicago office spent a lot of time finding partners for him. Every city boy sitting at an office desk thought he knew best what a man in the field needed.

While he was in town, he got together with Lorna once more. He hadn't really intended to do this, but he didn't fight much against it either. He only hoped that this time her perfume would wear off before he got back to the ranch. Rachel and Lorna had no liking for one another, and it ran a lot deeper than one being a Dowling and the other a Carter.

While he was there, Emma told him that Wild Margie had visited her and was now looking after her aunt. The old lady was so far gone she thought Margie was Emma and most of the time didn't notice she had been moved from her house. So when Ev came, Emma told him she was ready to leave with him for a new life farther west. She was all for riding out of town that very day. Ev hemmed and hawed for a while and finally said he didn't know whether he should go just yet.

"But you've been the one who's been pressing me to go all this time," she said, exasperated.

"I know, but when you wait things change."

"What's changed?"

"Gavin said so far as he was concerned, the ranch is mine."

"Sure. Just so long as he and the others can use it as a hideout."

"Reckon so," Ev said.

"You really want to stay, don't you?" she asked.

"I'm thinking about it, waiting to see."

"See what?"

"What's going to happen." he said.

In the midst of this peaceful lull at the ranch, Arthur and Martin rode in with a canvas bag of gold coins and a large jug of whiskey. Rachel went in her room and bolted the door. Gavin asked his two brothers how San Francisco had been, and they said just fine. He brought them up to date on the feud, and they said they had been intending to stay at Latrobe awhile, until they heard there about the new trouble at Wolf Creek and so had hurried on up. Gavin sure appreciated that. What were brothers for? they asked. They all had to stick together. Then they got round to Raider. They agreed that the best thing he could do was light out of there as soon as possible, at sunup tomorrow at the latest. This was fine with Raider, so long as Gavin was coming with him. They didn't think they could spare Gavin to go with him, he was needed on the ranch.

Raider let that pass. But when Martin, well into the jug, began banging on Rachel's door, demanding to be let in or he would break it down, the Pinkerton told him to ease up.

Martin crossed the kitchen to him. "This is our home, stranger. You don't walk in and tell a Dowling what to do in his own home."

"Leave her alone," Raider said.

Martin was about ready to go for his gun.

"Don't," Gavin warned.

Martin heeded his eldest brother and went back to the kitchen table, where Arthur passed him the jug and said something about waiting till tomorrow. The two men were travel weary and, after a short while, they sacked out on a corn-husk mattress in a spare room.

Raider slept in the barn. Ev came out the next morning with a plate of food and a mug of coffee.

"So I'm eating out with the horses now? No room at the kitchen table?"

"It ain't easy to eat in there," Ev said. "They're at the jug again, catching up before last night's effects wear off. They reckon the simplest thing might be to shoot you and bury you out back. Arthur kind of disagrees. He says they should shoot you and bring you into town and say the Carters done it, you being a friend of theirs. Rachel sent me out with this food. She thinks you should saddle up and stay at the hotel in town—not at the eating house."

Raider grinned. "You tell her I'll do what she says. You'll take care of her?"

"She'll be all right," Ev said. "She knows how to handle all of them. If anything, she'll take care of me."

The Pinkerton left without saying goodbye. He knew when he was outgunned, and in this particular case he didn't much care, since he needed another couple of days anyway before he would be ready to escort Gavin south to the railroad as his prisoner. A couple of days at the hotel in Bladen would make a pleasant change from the ranch life he had been living.

He met no one on the way into town and took a room at R. R. Quickley's Hotel, had a drink, went to the barber for a shave, then had some more drinks and joined a low-stakes poker game. He was ten dollars ahead when he quit to go to supper at the eating house.

Lorna said, "I heard you was in town."

"Room fourteen at the hotel."

"It wouldn't do for a respectable woman like me to be seen going in there alone or with you.'

"I guess that's why they don't lock the back door."

After Raider left the ranch for Bladen, Ev carried his empty plate and mug back into the house.

"That Pinkerton run off?" Gavin inquired.

Ev nodded.

They all laughed, and Gavin said, "We figured you'd pass the word to him he wasn't welcome around here no more. I figure he'll stop off at the hotel in Bladen a few days, hoping to grab ahold of me when my back is turned."

Ev said nothing, wishing to give them no information. Since Martin and Arthur had arrived, Gavin had taken to treating him like the family outcast once more.

"Well, he can stay at that hotel as long as he likes," Martin said. "In a couple of days he won't find hide nor hair of you, Gavin."

Gavin winked at him to warn him he was saying too much. The three men rose from the table, Gavin saying, "I'll ride on ahead and get some of the boys together. You know where we'll meet."

Over by the stove, Ev asked Rachel, "Where are they going?"

"I think they're going to rustle Carter cattle," she said.

"That don't make sense. They'll be tracked down easy before they get anyplace, and the brands will give them away. They ain't even stealing them at night. Those three may be crazy, but they ain't dumb."

Some minutes later, as Arthur was going out the door with Martin, he called to Ev, "Gavin wants you to stay here and watch the place."

"Where are you boys headed?" Ev asked casually.

"Not far. We'll be back for supper."

Once the door closed after them, Rachel commented, "They'll be back. They left the gold here behind them. I guess that's what they really want you to watch."

"But they're going to be long gone in a couple of days, Gavin at least. I hope all three of them go and don't come back. Rachel, I ain't sending word of this to Raider. I don't think even he expects me to inform on my own brothers."

"You're right, Ev," Rachel said, not mentioning the fact that Gavin was no brother of hers.

Gavin was waiting for Martin and Arthur with five young Dowling men, and they all rode together to where two of the young Dowlings had spotted big herds of Carter cattle. They were less than an hour out on the range when they came to a large herd grazing peacefully on rich grass.

"How many would you figure?" Gavin asked.

"Maybe eight hundred head," one of the young men said.

"How many head with Dowling brands?" Arthur asked.

"A few strays. Maybe a dozen, maybe twenty-five. Yesterday there was another herd just along a piece, about four hundred head. If we run these cattle that way, we can join the two herds."

"Let's do it," Gavin said. "You boys pick the point and flank riders from among yourselves. Me and my brothers will bring along the drag."

The five young Dowlings were flattered to be offered the choice positions of riding herd by these hardened veterans, forgetting that it had been years since Gavin and his brothers had controlled half-wild longhorns with half-broken cow ponies.

The steers began to move forward at a fast walk

after the riders took up positions around them. Within half an hour they had joined with the second herd, solved some leadership problems with their sharp horns, and moved at a steady clip east. The three brothers pulled bandannas up over their noses so they could breathe in the dust raised by the herd as they brought up the rear. At times the dust raised by the twelve hundred cattle was so thick and swirling they could see only a few yards in front of them. The grit got in their eyes, hair, and ears. In spite of the bandannas, dust got in their noses and their teeth bit on grit and their tongues were caked dry.

They kept the herd moving east at a steady pace, not wanting to tire the animals by running them at this stage. They knew that the huge column of dust rising in the sky behind the herd was a certain give-away and that a chase would be under way soon enough.

"If we can keep moving like this for another hour," Gavin yelled to Martin when their horses happened to come close together, "we have it made."

When at last the Carters did give chase, riding along the right flank, trying to cut off the herd and turn it back, nearly an hour had elapsed. The Dowlings shot at them, and the gunshots panicked the longhorns. The frightened animals stamped in the direction in which they had been traveling. Now they were impossible to cut off. Any horseman who came too close to them would risk being trampled, horse and all, or having one of his legs hooked by a sharp horn. The Dowlings whooped and hollered, shot in the air and at the Carters—anything to keep the herd stampeding.

At a fast walk, the herd had been only two hours

from the farmlands when they started the drive. Now they were less than fifteen minutes from them and running hard. The Dowlings kept up the pressure, and there was nothing the Carters could do about it, except fire at them and hope that a lucky shot would strike one of them as they galloped through the dust. These shots panicked the steers still further.

The herd burst through the barbed-wire fences as if they were no more than strands in a spider's web. They trampled the crops and rampaged across fields. The leaders swerved to avoid houses. However, one farmer's cabin was in their path. When the steers in front tried to avoid the plank cabin, the force and weight of the herd members behind pushed them on. Some animals were killed in the demolition of the cabin. Those that came after swarmed over them and trampled the lumber and carcasses underfoot. Gradually the tilled earth slowed the herd because of its soft and sticky going, but not until they had cut a long swathe of devastation through the farmland. By the time the herd slowed, the Dowlings were long gone and the Carters were left to reason with the irate farmers and round up the beasts as best they could.

Rachel had supper ready when they returned. She and Ev listened to what they had done as the three went over the events together, mighty pleased with themselves. Ev was quiet, watchful, and thinking. She said she'd had enough and was going visiting. Ev hitched a horse to the buggy for her and insisted that she take a light, single-barrel shotgun just in case, since the Carters must be tearing mad after what had happened. He offered to come with her, but she said no. He didn't ask where she was going, and she didn't tell him.

She was determined not to allow her fool cousin Gavin to create a full-scale war, even if she had to shoot him. And she could use a gun if she had to. But she had another way—get Raider after him quickly, before Gavin could do what he planned and make a getaway. She had no doubt that whatever it was that Gavin planned, he would leave them all behind to pay the price for it. She reasoned this all out very carefully as she drove along in the fading daylight toward Bladen. Naturally, all this would give her a chance to see Raider today, and the hour was already so late that there could be no question of her returning to Wolf Creek tonight.

Darkness fell when she was only halfway to town. She had been traveling this way since she was a little girl and had no doubt she would do all right in the dark. The horse was eleven years old, and probably could have managed without her. She cocked the shotgun and laid it across her thighs, then urged the horse on and kept up a more or less continuous stream of acid comments on its performance in order to pass the time.

After a long time and slow going, she saw the house lights of Bladen ahead. She drove straight to the hotel and tied the horse to the hitching post outside. In the lobby, the clerk sat with his face down on the desk, unmoving. Her heart skipped a beat. Then, even from where she stood, the strong smell of liquor suggested he might be only temporarily indisposed rather than dead. She pulled the guestbook out from under his head. Raider...Room 14. At this moment, she was grabbed from behind.

She shrieked as the strong hands seized her arms. She was immediately released, and one bony hand slithered down her back and patted her rump.

"Don't raise a holler, gal," a thick boozy voice said in her ear. "I'm only trying to be friends. Sure didn't mean to scare you none." He fell against her, pinning her between him and the reception desk.

Rachel put everything she had into her shove, and he went stumbling and careening across the lobby. He managed to stay on his feet and, thinking this was a hell of a lot of fun, started to chase her around the lobby. She thought about heading up the stairs, then decided that would really give this drunk the wrong idea. The only other way to go was out the door, which was better than standing screaming and making a laughingstock of herself in the town.

Outside she took the shotgun from under the seat. She tucked its butt under her right arm and headed in the lobby door again, barrel leveled straight ahead. She didn't cock the gun, figuring she would have plenty of time to do so and knowing that the sound of a hammer being cocked has brought many a man to his senses.

The drunk saw her come back in, but somehow he missed seeing the shotgun pointed at his belly, because he stuck out his arms and ran to grab her. Clearly the sound of a hammer being cocked would be lost on this specimen. She did the only thing a lady could do in the circumstances—she swung the gun by its barrel, whacked him with the butt across the side of the head, and stepped over him as he lay unconscious on the floor. After giving the passed-out hotel clerk a disapproving look, she ascended the stairs and knocked primly on the door of Room 14.

When there was no answer, she knocked again, more loudly.

"Gittaway!" a male snarled from inside the room.

"Raider, I know that's you. This is Rachel. Open the door instantly."

She was furious to hear a stream of muttered curses inside the room instead of a surprised and happy greeting. This caused her to reach a certain conclusion. "I know you have that Carter bitch in there! I swear I'll kill her! Open that door!"

Rachel let him hear her snap back the hammer.

Raider sprang into action when he recognized the sound of a shotgun being cocked. He draped a sheet around Lorna's naked body and led her to a tall closet with a mirrored door, which he held open as he urged her inside. He pushed her clothes, shoes, and purse in after her and closed the door. While he was hiking on his jeans and ignoring Rachel's comments in the corridor, Rachel grew so impatient that she pointed the shotgun barrel toward the hinged edge of the door and blew it into the room.

Raider was kind of surprised at this sudden development, and relieved that the shotgun had only one barrel.

"You caught me with my pants down, Rachel," he said to the woman glowering at him in the doorway, holding the smoking gun.

"Where is she?" Rachel asked.

"Who?"

"The Carter bitch." Rachel stepped onto the shattered door and off it onto the room carpet.

People were yelling down the corridor, and one brave soul was curious enough to peek in the doorway for a second. Rachel had forgotten about them.

"I know she's here," she was saying, looking about the room. "I can smell the vixen. Where have you hidden her?"

"You're doing me an injustice, Rachel," Raider said in a hurt voice.

She only laughed and stooped to look under the bed. This was the time Lorna chose to step out of the closet, half wrapped in her sheet, a derringer in her left hand. She took a fast shot at Rachel, who fortunately was still in the act of stooping, so that the bullet passed clean over her and clean through the wall into the next room, where it thumped into something.

First thing Raider registered was that the derringer was a single-shot model, and second that whatever the bullet had thumped into in the next room had made no sound—a good sign but not definite proof that it hadn't been a living creature of some sort.

"Have you any more shells for that gun?" Raider asked Lorna. She shook her head. "Have you any more cartridges?" he asked Rachel. She shook hers. "Well, that's a start anyway."

Two young men stood in the empty doorway, grinning at Lorna's scantily clad body. She hopped back in the closet and began putting on her clothes. Rachel quit cursing Lorna and started in on Raider, who was knocking on the wall near the bullet hole, asking if the next room's occupant was all right.

A curt, even male voice responded. "You better make your next shot in here count, fella, 'cause if you try again and miss, I'm going to empty a seventeen-shot magazine in your direction."

"He sounds in pretty good shape," Raider said, relieved.

Lorna stepped out of the closet with her clothes on. She said to Rachel, "Don't waste your time on this Pinkerton. No man is worth it. I need a drink."

"I'll join you," Rachel said, to Raider's amazement. He looked out the doorway after the two ladies walking down the corridor, still holding their weapons. Other guests were ducking back in their rooms and slamming their doors.

"I guess that's the last of them I'll see tonight," Raider muttered, surveying the damage. It made him smile to think of Allan Pinkerton's face when the Scotsman got the hotel bill for this.

He moved the shattered door across the floorboards with his foot. He had enemies out there—he needed to block that doorway. The closet would do. The closet at first resisted his efforts to move it, which puzzled him because it didn't seem all that heavy. Then it came loose as he wrenched it, and he realized it had been fixed to the wall with long screws. Some plaster and lathing were torn out along with the closet, which he dragged across the floor to the doorway.

"Keep it up, you crazy bastard!" an enraged voice yelled in the room beyond that wall. "What is it? The full fucking moon?"

# CHAPTER FOURTEEN

Ev was out on his horse before first light. Rachel hadn't come back. This wasn't all that unusual, since she often stayed over with cousins or friends, either at one of the ranches or in Bladen. Still and all, he was a little uneasy about her absence—though it seemed a wise move on her part, considering the state of his three brothers, who were all passed out on kitchen chairs.

First and foremost, Ev was a rancher—which meant that first and foremost on his mind were his cattle. It seemed reasonable to him to suppose that since the Dowling clan had broken the unspoken agreement not to harm each other's stock, the Carters would lose no time in getting back at Dowling herds. Like first thing this morning. He guessed his brothers had intended to be up and out early too, except that some whiskey got in the way of their plans. Ev didn't expect to hold off some Carter move on his own. He knew that most of the other Dowling families would have sense enough to have riders guarding their stock today. He would team up with them, since his cattle were mixed in with many of theirs. Ready to die defending his stock, Ev had totally forgotten that only a few days ago he had wanted to ride away and leave Wolf Creek forever.

Many of his steers were part of a big bunch just ahead, which had been strung out for more than a mile along this part of the range for the last few days. Anyone wanting to run a herd would find it easy to gather these animals. The steers were still bedded down on the grass, waiting for daylight. Ev could see very few of them in the poor light, but he knew from the sounds that most of the animals were still here and had not been disturbed during the night.

Ev was relieved to see a couple of Dowling boys riding herd on the stock. He called to them and they shouted back, easily so as not to spook the cattle. Ev wanted to hear their plans and feel assured at least that some of the others shared his worries about a Carter revenge raid on Dowling stock. Ev was aware that what struck him as plain common sense didn't always strike others in the same light. It was always better to talk with people and find out what was on their minds rather than depend on them to see things the same way as you.

He still wasn't sure which of the Dowling boys these were, and it wasn't until he was right close to them he saw Tommy Winthrop and Noah Carter. They were looking down the barrels of their .45s at him.

"Don't shoot him," Noah said.

"Why not?" Tommy asked. "This is the varmint who shot Phil Burke. I say give him a taste of his own medicine."

"I didn't shoot Phil," Ev said loudly.

"That's what you been claiming," Noah told him, "and I, for one, don't like it. You been spreading ugly rumors it was me and Tommy who done it. What gets me is there's some who believe it."

"Some people will believe anything," Tommy judged.

"Reckon so," Noah said. "I want those folks to hear from this dude's mouth that he done it himself."

Ev said, "You'll never put those words in my mouth."

"Won't we?" Noah said. "Me and Tommy have our ways."

They took Ev's rifle, tied his wrists, and led his horse at a lope toward Wolf Creek in the gathering light. They had crossed the creek before the sun pushed up on the horizon. It dawned on Ev that they were taking him to Emma's place—not by the series of draws and hollows that he used to take, but straight across by the shortest route. Once Noah and Tommy made it out of Dowling territory before daybreak, they had their captive where they wanted him. Emma's aunt had moved to Wild Margie's. The house would be empty now. Why were they taking him there?

They didn't take him to the house but instead to the barn, in the hayloft of which he had made love to Emma so many times. Was this now where he was going to die? A cold clammy fear, impossible for him to suppress or control, spread through Ev's mind.

In the barn, Tommy climbed up into the hayloft. As Ev had before, he picked up one of the coiled lariats stored there. He tossed the noose end down to

Noah, who tested the running knot and the strength of the braided rawhide while Tommy threw the other end over a freestanding rafter. Noah fitted the noose around Ev's neck, tightening it so the knot lay below his left ear. Tommy came down the ladder and pulled the rope taut across the rafter.

"This ain't no good," Tommy complained.

"It'll do for now," Noah said. "Don't make it too taut."

So long as Ev stood on the floor where he was, hands bound behind his back, there was no pressure on his neck. Noah punched him in the belly. Ev doubled over reflexively, but the rope caught him around the throat and choked him. This caused him to completely lose his balance, and he fell sideways. His neck might have snapped had not Tommy played out rope over the rafter as he went down. Ev's body weight dragged the rope over the rafter, which provided just enough friction to nearly strangle him but not enough to snap his vertebral column.

Noah loosened the noose around his neck as he lay on the floor, so he could breathe, and waited a minute so Ev's mind could clear.

"Stand up," Noah ordered. When Ev did not obey, Noah kicked him in the gut. Ev curled up like a fetus from the pain, his head not jerked back this time by the rope. His hands bound behind his back left his front totally open to any kind of attack Noah took a notion to. Ev tried to keep his knees tucked up to his chest as long as possible, and, in spite of the pain, which made him want to scream and beg for mercy, he feigned semiconsciousness in the hope they would leave him alone.

Noah wasn't fooled. "Ev, I know you can hear me. Stand up or I'll boot you again."

Ev needed Noah's help to get on his feet. As soon as he was upright, Tommy drew the rope over the rafter until it was taut again.

"You think he's ready to talk, Tommy?" Noah asked.

"Hell no, he's Gavin's brother," Tommy said. "He's so tough we're going to have to bust things inside him before he'll even listen to us. I bet we end up having to hang him 'cause he won't talk with us."

"I'll talk!" Ev croaked.

"You see?" Noah said. "I knew he'd be reasonable."

Tommy said in a scoffing way, "He ain't said nothing I want to hear yet."

"What do you want to talk about?" Ev asked in a hoarse voice, his throat still recovering from being squeezed by the lariat.

"Who killed Phil Burke?" Noah asked.

There was a pause.

"I'd be a fool to say I did," Ev claimed, "especially when I didn't."

"Bring over that stool, Tommy," Noah commanded.

Tommy placed it next to Ev and went back to his end of the rope. Ev thought he was going to be asked to stand on the stool. He felt the end was near.

"Well, sit down," Noah said.

Ev waited for Tommy to give him slack, then sat on the stool.

"You know us, Ev. We went to school together," Noah declared. "Phil and Emma too. We don't feel good about what happened to Phil, but he got what was coming to him for being a turncoat. All the same, people who liked him are blaming us for killing him. A lot of Carters are holding a grudge against us for it, and it's hard on Tommy and me. That's why we want to do a deal with you. You admit you killed Phil, and we'll let you go."

"I killed Phil," Ev said. "Now let me go."

Noah laughed. "Ev, you was always a smart-ass, and I know you're brainier than me or Tommy. Only your brains ain't going to get this noose from around your neck. If me or Tommy had the idea you were fooling us, we wouldn't waste no more time bargaining with you. We want you to admit it in front of some Carters. They'll want to hang you, but we'll say we can't do it till Toss is here. Nobody does nothing unless Toss Carter says all right. Before he gets here, we'll let you escape."

"Why would you let me escape?" Ev asked sardonically.

"For good reason. If we hung you, some Carters would say we forced the confession from you and then killed you because we're really the guilty ones. But if you get away, they'll see it different. Every Carter will be gunning for you. You'll be shot if you stay, or you'll run off with Emma and no one will ever see you two again. Either way, it's fine with me and Tommy. It gets us off the hook."

Ev admitted he saw the logic of this. They told him he would be stood on the stool at sundown but his wrist bonds would be cut, unknown to the others. They brought him outside and tied a horse for him to a bush in a hollow, a roan mare in fine fettle.

"Dark will be coming on," Noah said. "You'll make it out of here."

Ev nodded. He said nothing about the line of draws and hollows in which he could disappear in minutes and which he knew like the back of his hand.

Tommy said, "Either we have a deal or we string you up right now."

"We have a deal," Ev said.

Raider knew it was trouble for sure when he saw Emma rush into the saloon. He was a big man, and it never took a woman long to find him in a crowd. He waited for her to get to him, savoring a last peaceful glass of whiskey before trouble hit. A couple of days of healthful rest in Bladen's saloons was too much to ask for in these parts.

Wild Margie had sent a kid into town with word to Emma that Ev was to be hanged today at sundown. Margie said Emma should come back quick to try to save him. He was to be strung up in her barn.

"Whose kid is this?" Raider asked.

"What does it matter?" Emma asked, half in hysterics.

"It matters," Raider said. "Maybe it's only a trick of Toss's to lure you back. We don't know they've taken Ev prisoner."

"I have to go, Raider. I have to go."

"No, you don't," he said. "I'm the one who has to go, Emma."

"You will? God bless you, Raider. We'll go together."

"No way, lady. One of us stays in town. Take your pick."

She tried to persuade him. She tried to lie to him.

He wouldn't move from the bar and kept refilling his glass.

She gave in. "I'll stay here with Lorna."

After leaving her with Lorna—who warned him, "Stay away from that Dowling cow!"—Raider headed out of town at a short lope and made it to the ranch in way less than three hours, with maybe an hour to sundown. He tied his horse to the corral rail, drew his .44, and, in full view of the house, tipped the loads out of the chambers into his left palm.

Then he walked up to the door and shouted, "They got Ev and they're set on hanging him at sundown. I'm going over that way myself. I thought you might want to come along."

The house door burst open and Gavin, Martin, and Arthur came running out with rifles, shotguns, cartridge belts, and bloody oaths. Raider grinned. It wasn't all bad having family like this. They were saddled and riding out of there in two minutes, following Raider into the draws that led to Emma's place. Rachel stood looking after them in the doorway, tears running down her face.

Being reasonable himself, Ev persuaded himself that Noah and Tommy would keep their part of the deal. Of course a man with his hands tied behind his back and his neck in a noose, even if he is sitting on a stool, needs to persuade himself that he still has hope. Ev needed to believe. The first blow to that belief was the sight of the roan mare running free in the corral. This was the horse that had been tied in the hollow for him. Maybe someone had found the mare there by chance and brought her to the corral. That had to be it. Tommy and Noah kept their distance from him, now that others were around, so he had no chance to tell them. With all the excitement, they probably hadn't noticed that the mare was now in the corral.

Some of the Carters spat at him, others slapped or punched him. Some looked him in the eye and said nothing, slow to be convinced. After first telling some of them he had killed Phil Burke, Ev refused to say another word. The words stuck in his throat. If he had wanted to, he could no longer have managed to say them.

As soon as Toss Carter arrived, he would be hung. A number of people told him that. Toss was expected at sundown. Some folks told him to enjoy that sundown, since it was the last one he would ever see. It began to dawn on Ev that he had made a bad mistake in falsely confessing to Phil's killing. Those who had heard him confess told others—it was no longer Tommy and Noah's version of events versus his. Before this, even the Carters had a low opinion of Tommy and Noah, and a higher opinion of him. Through his own words, Ev had destroyed this. Tommy and Noah didn't need to let him escape now. They could let him hang. But Ev looked on himself as smarter than those two. He couldn't accept that maybe they had hoodwinked him in a sly way. He still insisted on believing they would stick by their bargain.

Word came that Toss was delayed. He was sorry to miss it, but go ahead with the hanging.

They stood Ev on the stool, checked the noose around his neck, tautened the rope over the rafter, tied down its loose end, then drew for high card to see who would have the privilege of kicking the stool out from beneath his feet. Noah and Tommy kept their distance. They didn't even draw cards. No one severed his bonds.

It finally dawned on Ev. "I didn't do it," he said. "I made a deal with Noah and Tommy. They promised to free me if I confessed."

He looked at the upturned faces of the men on the barn floor, spotting a few that might have believed him, but none so strongly that they were going to stop what was about to happen. Noah and Tommy stood at a distance, their backs to the wall, looking every which way but at him. The holder of the high card showed it to the crowd and sauntered up to kick away the stool. Ev tried to keep his eyes open, his face rigid, and his mouth shut. He thought he might piss in his pants, but he wanted to die like a man.

"Don't none of you bastards move or I'll blow you to hell," Wild Margie shouted down from the hayloft, covering the men with her single-barrel scattergun. "I got a load of deershot in here that'll tear you to pieces. You with the knife, cut that man down. Run, Ev, run. Anyone tries to go after him, I swear I'll smear you on the barn wall."

Being far back, Tommy and Noah slipped out before she could cover them.

Raider lost his way in the draws and hollows after they crossed Wolf Creek. "To hell with it," he said. "It's near enough sundown, let's take the fast way even if it means we'll be seen."

This time Gavin took the lead. After a spell he asked Martin if he knew the way, and Martin had to ask Arthur. All of them had been away so often and so long, things looked different now to them. Besides, they hadn't been in Carter territory all that often at any time. In other words, none of them were sure exactly where Emma's place was—they knew the general direction but not the exact spot.

This was news to Raider, who had assumed these local boys would know at least this. Seeing some familiar landmarks, he at last guided them there. They were too late now to conceal the horses and sneak up on the place. The sun was setting. The four of them rode in.

As Raider rode in the lead between the ranch house and the barn, he met Ev running out the barn door, his hands tied behind his back, trailing a length of hanging rope from his neck. Raider brought his horse alongside the running man, reached down behind him, and lifted him by the armpits to throw him belly down across the front of his saddle.

This move, and the added weight, slowed horse and rider down. They were an easy target for the .45s of Noah and Tommy, less than fifteen yards away. Both dove for their guns.

A hail of shotgun, rifle, and revolver lead cut them down before their revolvers cleared leather. Martin emptied both barrels of his shotgun into them, and Gavin the six shots of his Peacemaker, while Arthur kept half his Winchester magazine in reserve, not having time to lever seventeen shots. None of them missed.

# CHAPTER FIFTEEN

"Emma must have told Wild Margie, when she went to visit her in Bladen, about the back way into the barn. I built it out of old lumber and leaned it against the side of the barn, so it didn't look like nothing. It was my escape route if something went wrong. Nothing ever did till now."

"Is Margie going to be all right?"

Ev laughed. "All those men there are going to be so ashamed to be caught like that by a woman, tomorrow you won't hear one of them admit it. Whoever they blame, it won't be Margie."

He was riding behind Raider as they neared the ranch, along with his three brothers.

Gavin rode close and said, "You better ride south with us, Ev. We're taking a herd down with some Dowling boys."

"I figured that's why you ran the Carter stock," Ev said bitterly. "You're going to sweep our ranch clean of stock too after I built up something that could hold us all together. I see now why you said I could have this ranch. There ain't going to be nothing on it 'cept jackrabbits."

"If you come along, you'll get your cut," Gavin promised.

"Is that what our Dowling kin believe, the fools willing to join their animals with ours and drive them south with you? You ain't going to cheat them? I'm going nowhere with you three."

"You're a dead man if you stay on here," Gavin said and left it at that. He paid no heed to Raider, and Raider said nothing about Gavin's plan.

At the ranch, Ev jumped down to open the corral for their horses and waved to Rachel, weeping now with joy at the house door.

Martin and Arthur steered their horses into the corral. Gavin found himself looking into Raider's Remington .44. The Pinkerton had pulled Gavin's Peacemaker and rifle before anyone properly noticed.

Raider said nice and quiet, "I reckon you folks won't be needing us two from now on. We'll be on our way."

He looked Martin and Arthur over like he was inviting them to go for their guns. The moon had only just begun to rise, but with their eyes accustomed to the dark and with the light from the house, they could all see each other as much as they needed.

"He's got the drop on us," Gavin continued. "Let him take me. Rest up a spell, then come after us. While he has me with him, he'll get no sleep."

They watched in silence as the Pinkerton and his prisoner rode out into the darkness.

• • •

Toss Carter was in a foul mood. He had stayed away from Ev Dowling's hanging deliberately, because so many Carters were believing Ev innocent of killing Phil and not believing Tommy and Noah. Some Carter womenfolk were even openly saying they saw no reason why Ev shouldn't marry Emma. Toss knew better than to make an open stand against popular opinion—he would fix things so they went his way. Having Ev hung in his absence was part of that. But no one could get a thing done right when he wasn't there to watch. They messed up a simple hanging. This put Toss in a bad mood.

He gathered a bunch of men and rode by moonlight over to Gavin Dowling's place, intending to hit them so quickly they would be surprised even though they would be expecting trouble. A scout he had sent earlier rode back to tell him that the Pinkerton had already ridden off with Gavin. This news made Toss stop and think. Martin and Arthur would never let him take Gavin prisoner. Had the Pinkerton killed them both? Toss feared Arthur and Martin almost as much as he did Gavin, and he didn't want to take any action without knowing their condition and whereabouts.

"Let's take a look," he decided.

He had the men spread out and keep their horses still, so they wouldn't be seen. They watched the ranch house for a spell. When they saw nothing, they came in closer, then closer. The Carter horsemen were standing motionless in the gray shadows of moonlight when two men came out of the ranch house. One carried a lamp, and by its light Toss saw that they were Martin and Arthur. The two men went to the corral to catch their horses.

As they climbed the rails, Toss raised his rifle to his shoulder, sighted on Martin's belly button, and squeezed the trigger. The bullet lifted Martin off the top corral rail and threw him quivering on his back in the dirt. He had taken the slug in his lower chest. Blood trickled from his mouth. He was going fast.

A half-dozen Carter riflemen fired on Arthur before he could get away from the lamplight. Only one shot hit him, but it was enough. He collapsed in the dirt beside his brother.

Ev began firing on the Carters from the ranch house. The light was tricky, and he was no marksman; they had nothing to worry about.

"To hell with him," Toss said, feeling flushed with victory. "The two we want now is that Pinkerton and Gavin."

"Let them go, Toss," one man said. "Gavin will swing for sure, and I for one don't want to mess with Raider."

There was a chorus of assenting voices to this—cut of by Toss. "You men take care of Gavin, then. Leave the goddamn Pinkerton to me. I'll nail him."

A voice called out from behind them in the still night air. "Then you won't have far to look, Toss. Here I am."

Toss Carter nearly fell off his horse with fright. "How'd you get here?" he yelled.

"I figured Arthur and Martin would try to follow, so I doubled back, waiting for them to be ahead. That way they would be easy to lose. Gavin's here, trussed to his horse, a bandanna stuffed in his mouth. Any man of you who fires on a helpless man like him will swing for cold-blooded murder, you have my word on that."

None of them said anything to that. Raider came closer, trailing Gavin's horse on a rope from his saddle.

"Now, I heard one man speak good sense when he said you-all should let us ride away. Seems you're the main one disagreeing with that, Toss."

Toss couldn't back down in front of his kinfolk. "I am."

"I don't want you back-shooting me," the Pinkerton said. "You go home and sit quiet or throw some lead in my face right now. That's right, I'm challenging you."

Toss Carter saw the choice he had. He could go home and play with his grandchildren, no longer leader of the Carter clan, or he could chance dying with his boots on. Right now.

The Pinkerton calmly waited. The Carters showed no sign of turning on him as a mob. They weren't even looking at the Pinkerton. They were looking at Toss to see what he would do.

Toss made his choice. He slid his rifle back in its saddle scabbard and, in one smooth motion, whipped out his Colt .45 from its holster.

The Pinkerton's long-barrel Remington .44 spoke with a spurt of flame. The range was more than forty yards, but a single bullet did the work. Toss Carter took it in the mouth, and it stove in his toothless upper jaw. A cousin caught him before he fell from the saddle and, with the help of others, secured his corpse to the horse. The bunch of men rode toward Wolf Creek without another word.

Ev was at the corral, checking on Martin and Arthur. Rachel stood in the house doorway.

"They've both passed on," Ev said in a voice that surprised Raider by its regretfulness.

"You're better off without them, and without this one here," Raider said, pulling the bandanna out of Gavin's mouth.

"Maybe," Ev answered, "but they're all I got as close family."

Gavin smiled. "You're on your own now, Ev. This place is yours. Raider here is a witness. I'm giving it to you. You'd best marry Emma like you want and make peace with the Carters. You're the one who can do it. All you cattlemen are going to need to stand together against them damn farmers. Of course I may hide out here from time to time when my lawyer gets me off these charges. Or maybe I'll kill this dumb Pinkerton on the way. Well, take care, Ev. Remember me sometimes."

Raider nodded to Ev and began to move out.

Ev shouted after him, "When you pass through Bladen, tell Emma I'm all right."

This roused Rachel at the door. "Stay away from the other Carter bitch at that eating house!"